Me, Margarita:
Stories

Ana Kordzaia-Samadashvili

Translated by
Victoria Field and Natalia Bukia-Peters

DALKEY ARCHIVE PRESS
Champaign / London / Dublin

CONTENTS

AN INTERVIEW WITH
ANA KORDZAIA-SAMADASHVILI

The title story suggests that the final Margarita has had things "happening to her for centuries [...] she was under the influence of generations of 'Margaritas.'" How does this image, one which is central to the story, apply to the whole collection—and more broadly to Georgia?

Certainly I think the existence of all the previous Margaritas conditions each Margarita. It is clear that if it was not for the three wars after the nineties, the first and the second world wars, the Soviet Union etc., we would have been entirely different. But not better or worse, just we would have been different.

Working against this image—probably the most frequently used phrase in the collection is "to cut a long story short." Is there an irony here in that this is what this collection is trying to do—cut the long story of Georgian history, and women's experiences of it, short, and condense it into fiction?

It comes from Rustaveli's poem *The Knight in the Panther's Skin*— "the long word can be said shortly" ... besides, nothing so important is happening as to require a long narration. It's just a matter of form, that's all.

Probably the next most used phrase, one that peppers the dialogue of so many characters in the collection, is "so what?" How much is this the writer of fiction reflecting on her efforts and wondering what it's for; how much of this is the ennui of the twenty-first century, post–Soviet experience; and finally how much is it a question for the reader: how should

7

she respond to this documentation of the Georgian female experience?

I would say the following: in relation to eternity, it can be said, so what? It is a matter of experience. Whatever does not kill us strengthens our health. Certainly it is again the matter of time, the time when these women live, but I don't think it deserves any other evaluation. I am not trying to be cynical, no, it is just that I really think like that.

When did you begin writing fiction? Was it something you always wanted to do or did you feel it was something you "must" do?

I started writing late, when I was over thirty. It was for a German architectural magazine, *Stadtbauwelt*, which produced a special edition dedicated to Tbilisi. I translated some pieces for this magazine and they also asked me to write some original articles. They paid me so well that I got the idea that it was a good way of making money! I was naïve. Nobody in Georgia ever got rich by writing, but I enjoyed it. That's how my writing career began, in an ordinary way. The very first stories I had published in a newspaper were a success. I received the Saba award for 'Newcomer of the Year'.

Obviously, I was very pleased and I carried on writing. My second collection, *Me, Margarita*, became a best-seller and I was happier. Having said that, it was never my intention to become a writer. I knew that my command of the Georgian language was very good and I always loved telling stories, but I never thought about actually writing. It wasn't a dream of mine. I wanted to be a gardener or a singer. When I was young they predicted that I would become a ballerina. I did translations and so on, but writing was the last thing I had ever thought about. I loved reading but not writing. I just somehow fell into it. Also, the man I loved thought my writing was the best thing about me. The man is gone but I have to keep writing.

What's your sense of the "writing scene" in Georgia now? Lively and active? From the outside, we see Georgia as a kind of "hot bed" of very interesting writers, ones that we very much want to translate and publish into English. This is not always the case with all countries.

My generation has seen and experienced so much that it would be enough for three generations. The Soviet Union collapsed, then there was a civil war, then a second one and three more wars, in quick succession. And our literature reflects, above all, the huge lust for life and its joys, which our generation still has. We are at the beginning of something because, as I understand it, it usually takes at least ten years to come to terms with living under capitalism. The first outstanding example of Georgian literature dates back to the fifth century. Georgians began with the novel form straight away, the passionate description of events, an absolutely crazy text, and because my people have long memories, the nation remains faithful to this tradition to this day. Over the past twenty years, in this tiny country, in this tiny language, some magnificent pieces of literature have been created. They are full of the desire for life and happiness. Here, it doesn't work to say, I love it "a bit," I want it "a bit." We want, we love, we kill, we sing and we do everything to the full.

Is it important to you to have your fiction translated into English? If so, why?

It's certainly very important. In other words, I am very happy that my girls are everywhere. If the concerns of my Margaritas are read about in different countries and in different languages, let them be joyful knowing that they are not alone. Let them remember that somewhere in a faraway country, there's a railway station called Margarita, and what is it—finding just one station?

INTRODUCTION

Translation has been a feature of our shared life and work since we became friends at first sight over fifteen years ago. Significantly, perhaps, we met in Cornwall, a small country, culturally distinct from England, brought together by a shared interest in Russian. Natalia is a native-speaker of Russian and Victoria lived for a few years in Moscow in the early '90s, during which time she regularly visited Georgia. Maybe we crossed in the street back then, but those were the war-torn years when the hotels were full of refugees, power and water supplies were intermittent, gunshots rang out at night, and, not surprisingly, social encounters tended to be private and domestic.

Since we met, we've spent a lot of our time together translating formally and informally. This involves working on stories and poems, but also the more holistic translation that any cross-cultural relationship requires. Each of us attempts to explain her culture to the other, trying to convey what it means to be a Georgian woman who has lived a long time in Cornwall, or an Englishwoman who sees Georgia through a glass darkly, based on infrequent visits, on friendships and on books.

Specifically, we engage in the painstaking work of trying to make a sentence in English evoke in an unknown, unseen reader—in, say, Canada, Sydney or Edinburgh—the same experience as the original Georgian sentence did in Tbilisi, Batumi or Poti.

Georgian is not an Indo-European language, so this effort comes with particular technical difficulties. There are no genders, which leads to ambiguities that can be variously intriguing or frustratingly vague. All the stories in this collection are in the first person, and there are plenty of clues that this person is usually female.

One of the stories, though, has no such pointers, and the reader can, as we did, experience the speaker of the story as a man or a lesbian woman. Eventually, context suggested—to us at least—that the narrator of 'Tbilisi. November 2004' is male.

There is a similarly absent binary distinction with regard to articles: there are none in Georgian. The house or a house? Some houses or the houses? Again, much depends on how we picture someone experiencing a house. Ana Kordzaia has a particular interest in houses and their histories, and they feature strongly in many stories.

Another transpositional difficulty we encounter is that a single Georgian verb can convey several English words: for example the English 'they made her jump' is simply *tsamoakhtunes* in Georgian.

The Russian language has had a big influence on Georgian. Sometimes, Russian phrases and proverbs have been transformed into a specific Georgian jargon. Ana Kordzaia also uses colloquialisms specific to Western Georgia and specific generations and social groups. For example, in the title story, 'Me, Margarita,' the word *chatakhtuli* is used for sofa, in place of the more usual *takhti*. In Western Georgia, a *chatakhtuli* is not simply a sofa, but one with a rug that comes down from the ceiling to cover it—the longer the rug, the more prestigious the family. Tantsia, one of the main characters in the story, is very proud of her sofa, and even more proud of the rug given to her by the Lady Margarita. The simple English word 'sofa' can't fully convey the reasons for Tantsia's pride. Fortunately, we were able to discuss many such nuances with Ana.

Names in Georgian, as in Russian, pose particular challenges. There are usually numerous diminutives, familiar to Georgian readers, but potentially confusing for an English reader. All four women in the title story are called Margarita, but in various versions; and Margarita is sometimes referred to as Margalita by

Tantsia, who, although she was baptised Margarita, is named for the railway station. In another story, 'It's Raining,' the name Toma is a diminutive of Tamara. In 'Dombrovsky,' it's significant that Erik can't understand that the Polish woman should be called Dombrovska, the feminine version of her surname, differentiated from her father's surname. In 'Autumn and That Lovely Man,' the narrator's friend calls herself variously Nikoliko, Nikol, Nick and Nickipore, depending on her mood and reflecting her desire to sound androgynous. We sometimes chose to use names more consistently for the sake of clarity.

Communicating the territory Kordzaia covers in this collection has been a more uneven experience. Displacement is a recurring theme in these stories. The protagonists are often in unspecified Western or former Soviet countries. In 'Dombrovsky,' the eponymous speaker is a Polish woman who has traveled to the West to find her fortune. She indeed finds success, fulfilling the dreams of her family, who'd gathered their last pennies in order for her to study in Germany. The story is humorous and easy to comprehend. Its themes of immigration, mixed marriages, and cross-cultural relationships are relevant in many societies and are a particular feature of Europe in recent years. The finale of the story describes the ecstatic joy of the only Polish wedding guest with some knowledge of German. He toasts Pani Dombrovsky, expressing pride in her marriage and, at the same time, pride in the Polish village they all come from. He is convinced everyone knows where it is.

However, the story 'Expecting the Barbarians' was much more difficult to render into English. The humour is specifically Georgian, and, as well as linguistic challenges, the story assumes familiarity with the cultural and political turmoil in Georgia during the nineties, after the collapse of the Soviet Union, when different sectors of society either accepted or resisted changes to their ways of life. The humour is bittersweet, describing the misery of those Tbilisi-ites who were inflexible and lamented the safe Soviet past, and, on the other side, more progressive non-Tbilisi-ites adapting easily to the challenges of the capitalist system, irritating their compatriots who seem to be dozing in a fantasy of the past. One character, Zhora, is an Armenian native of Tbilisi, who cannot and will not accept outsiders, even though they are Georgians. His monologues constantly rail against so-called provincials—those unsophisticated people from outside Tbilisi. He expresses his love for Stalin, hatred of Khrushchev, and confusion about Zviad Gamsakhurdia, the first president of post-Soviet Georgia. He speaks a mixture of grammatically incorrect Georgian and Russian, his sentences full of inappropriate double negatives.

Many of Ana Kordzaia's stories explore relationships between men and women in Georgian society and beyond, often describing the bitterness of failed love, disappointment, and unfulfilled expectations. Ana has a particular take on this universal theme, which had an impact on our translation. She uses sexual imagery and profane language, painting the most vivid of pictures to give strong voices to female characters, who are often independent and sometimes bohemian. In 'It's Raining,' for example, the narrator appears, in very colourful terms, to despise the subservient, unimaginative Toma, who is dedicated to her callous husband. Here the challenge was to honour the strong language while not alienating the reader.

Other stories have a distinct and different voice. The story, 'There, In the North' describes with great tenderness the friendship between a small girl and a psychiatric patient: the child's tiny toothbrush and her naive fear of being beaten for wetting herself. In contrast, in 'With Love to the Man Whom I Love the Most' the crude and strong language and dark humor convey the bitterness of the man-woman relationship at its heart.

The difficulty of finding sustained love is explored again in 'Berikaoba,' the title referring to an ancient fertility festivity with its promise of love and happiness. Yet again, society limits the possibility of ultimate fulfilment.

Natalia found the story 'Tbilisi. November 2004' especially hilarious for its foreigner's take on Georgia. The story is in the form of the diary entries of a Swedish artist visiting the country. His impressions echo those of most Westerners coming to Georgia for the first time: their love-hate reactions and the confusion they express in the face of a complex society, its culture and politics. Sensitive political issues, such as the war in Chechnya, and social customs, such as going to the bathhouse, drinking to excess, and the impossibility of really knowing what people think, are all explored with a light touch.

We found this project both a challenge and highly enjoyable. Georgia is little-known in the international scene and news reports are inevitably top-down and focused on the sensational. Fiction can give a more nuanced picture of a society that has undergone extraordinary transitions over the past decades, and contemporary writers, especially, provide a snapshot of a complex and constantly changing world. Ana Kordzaia's focus on women, the domestic, and the minutiae of relationships, gives a bottom-up perspective on Georgian experience. We hope we have risen to the challenge of finding an English equivalent to her unusual, strong and sometimes elliptical prose so the reader can enter fully into the world she describes. We would like to thank Dalkey Archive for this opportunity.

—**Natalia Bukia-Peters & Victoria Field**

Me, Margarita:
Stories

ME, MARGARITA

There's a gorge, a very beautiful one, that probably everyone in Georgia has visited at one time or another. During the last century, it changed hands many times. First, a Sultan got hold of it, then some Persians, and, after that, the Turks again. Later, Paskevich invaded Akhaltsikhe, which was under the governance of the Ottomans, and claimed the gorge as the property of Russia. The Georgian princes sold it on the spot.

It was during the period of Russian rule that some lucky person discovered the natural mineral waters there. A few years later, the Georgian Grenadiers cleared a path through the thick forest to the springs. They put up some pretty buildings and, very soon, the gorge became full of life, attracting many visitors.

In 1871, the area came under the rule of the Supreme Governor, Mikhail Nikolaevich, and, however ridiculous it sounds, I must thank whoever handed it over for providing my ancestors with an identity. Everyone around me seems to know what their grandfathers' fathers were called, but I don't. I only know that Supreme Governor Mikhail Nikolaevich was ultimately—if involuntarily—responsible for my birth. Without him, Mikhail-Gavriil would never have gotten a job pouring mineral water into bottles, and nor would plump Tantsia have gone to the springs to sell her pies. And nor would the two of them have been able to communicate with each other, as they would not have had Russian as their common language.

1.

Although nearly forty years had passed since the Supreme Governor first appeared in the area, his story hadn't been forgotten in the gorge. The palace certainly remained; the narrow gorge was called Prince's Water; two men were known as the Great Princes, and a little girl was given the nickname 'Tantsia.' The name means 'dance' in Russian, but she wasn't called that because of the dances and entertainment that occurred at that time. She was in fact named in honour of the Great Prince's arrival at the railway station, where there was a sign saying 'station,' the Russian for which sounds a bit like 'Tantsia.'

Tantsia was raised by local aristocrats in their own household. No one knows why. She may have been an orphan, or perhaps her mother was a housemaid. The main thing is that she was brought up properly and that's why she was able to read and write. She could speak a little Russian, which in that village was a big deal. In addition, these aristocrats gave Tantsia their surname, and when she got married, provided a dowry. That was an act of great generosity, especially at that time, when even the gentry were shamefully impoverished.

Tantsia was beautiful, petite, fair-haired, with large breasts; and, for a poor woman, unusually proud.

She was always neatly dressed, and, when the sun was scorching hot, she would wear a scarf over her face to avoid getting burned and damaging her skin.

She kept her house in a similar fashion. It was cosy and polished like a new penny. She was very proud of her house and particularly of her sofa. She covered it with a rug that had the date '1910' stitched in one corner. It had been given to her by Lady Margarita as a wedding present. Tantsia constantly told people that the rug had been woven especially for her. The thing is, though, the date was a bit of a giveaway. It was neither the year of her birth, nor the year of her marriage. She would have been three or four years old by then, so who knows who this rug was originally woven for. The main thing is that, at the time when our story begins, the rug, along with propaganda posters for collective farms, adorned the tiny house where Tantsia lived alone. She was widowed but nevertheless was as proud and plump as she was in the old days. It wasn't for nothing that they said in the gorge that Tantsia was a true lady, like one painted in a portrait.

The man to whom Tantsia had been married at one stage had problems. No, he wasn't particularly poor, it was just that, embarrassingly, his manhood was often whispered about. Besides, he was a thief. He stole and didn't care what. It could be a pumpkin hanging on a neighbour's fence, or mineral water in a dark green bottle. Such water was so abundant in that area, no one knew what to do with it; in fact generally there wasn't much worth stealing around there. But he stole anyway, and after he'd done it, that night he'd feel remorseful. He would sit on the sofa and wake up poor Tantsia. She would hastily light the flickering oil lamp and he would begin his repentance by wailing and keening. Of course, he didn't possess an icon, so he wailed at the posters with their images of newly grown pumpkins and thick-legged women, and the slogan, 'The Anniversary of the Patronage of the Fleet by the Regional Committee of Young Communists,' only he didn't know what that meant. It was also a difficult phrase for Tantsia to understand.

The next day, he would steal again. Sometimes, he got caught and was beaten up. At other times, he got away with it; either way, he would wail at night. One day he was caught red-handed in a hut where someone was storing millet, and it seems they thrashed him with excessive violence. He was found at dawn, dead near Prince's Water. In fact, it wasn't the beating that killed him, although no one really knows what caused his death. They buried him near the oak trees where, in pre-Soviet times, there'd been a blue wooden church with a golden dome. Lady Margarita used to say that the church was dedicated to her angel, but no one knows whether or not that was really true.

So, that's how Tantsia came to be widowed and left alone. She mourned for a while—after all, that's what widows usually do—and then she went back to living as before.

***

On the whole, Tantsia wasn't a worrier. She wasn't bothered by the Revolution, nor by the Great War, nor the Second World War. During those years, nothing much changed in her life. The aristocrats moved away into town, and afterwards they disappeared somewhere. Only Lady Margarita, or Lord Margalita as Tantsia called her, still came in the summer. There weren't many men left in the village, but Tantsia never thought about that. She was interested neither in village life, nor in men. Her world was a tiny one, limited to the gorge itself: for her that was quite sufficient.

Later, when the Second World War was over, holidaymakers started coming to the springs, foreign faces appeared, and new opportunities for work materialised—men were given jobs bottling the mineral water, and women started selling and exchanging all kinds of small things. Tantsia got involved as well. Every other day, she would put pies made out of potatoes into Lord Margalita's basket, cover them with an embroidered handkerchief, hang the basket on her arm, and mince off to the waters. She didn't do it to earn money but in order to mingle with people. If you asked her in the evening what she was doing at the waters, she probably wouldn't be able to tell you, she wouldn't remember. She simply went there and that was that.

Once, when Tantsia 'simply went there,' something happened. It was only afterwards that she wondered whether the consequences were ultimately good or bad. At the time, she only understood that something had happened. She hadn't yet reached the waters when she slipped on the hillside and fell over, in precisely a manner inappropriate for a woman like her, that's to say, awkwardly. The worse thing was that everyone, both locals and outsiders, was watching her. She was so flustered that it was only later that she noticed what bad luck she'd had: the handle of the basket had come off and her beautiful pies were scattered all over the road.

Of course, people rushed towards her, expressing their concern all over the place. Tantsia smiled, embarrassed, and tried to hide her mud-covered hands. The problem was she didn't know what to do with the basket and the pies, so she decided to behave as befits a woman brought up by aristocrats; in other words, she abandoned them. She put the damaged pies back into the basket, and although she felt regretful, she left the basket at the side of the road. Then she shook out the handkerchief, tucked it up her sleeve and went home, strolling along ever so casually. But she felt self-conscious: she was able to walk more gracefully when she was carrying the basket.

To put it in a nutshell, something had happened that Tantsia couldn't forget. At the very least, she no longer had a basket, so she couldn't go to the waters anymore. She certainly couldn't go there awkwardly trying to carry pies in her lap! But this is only the beginning of the story because two days later, someone was calling at her fence.

'Hey, missus!'

It was a man! A stranger! Russian! With hair black as a beetle! With blue, blue eyes! He was holding a basket in his hand, not one like the one she was used to, but woven in a completely different style. The man was standing behind the fence, with one hand raised, and he was showing Tantsia the basket.

Tantsia's heart stopped. She couldn't breathe. She didn't know what to do. Should she invite him in? No, it would be unheard of to invite a stranger, especially a man, into the house! So, should she approach him? Oh, dear! But what if she couldn't understand his Russian? Tantsia stood and stared at him with her hand over her mouth.

The man looked at her too. He looked at her, and then put the basket down near the fence and left. He turned his head a few times, but nevertheless, eventually went on his way.

There was something in the basket, covered with mulberry leaves. Tantsia squatted down and removed them. And saw some prunes.

'Who was that man?' wondered Tantsia.

***

That man was Russian, and, at one stage, he lived in a different land, on the banks of a big river. When he was three days old, he'd been taken to a church and baptised. That was the custom in that country. A child was baptised immediately so that if he or she died, they would be received by God. It would be unheard of to give a Christian burial to anyone who hadn't been baptised! Of course, the man had been given a name, Gavriil. The thing is, though, his godfather had been totally pissed and his godmother too was just as drunk, and they instantly forgot the child's name. In order to save face when they got home, they told the parents that their son was called Mikhail.

So, he lived in the world as Mikhail, until the 1930s, when he was one of those to be deported. They pulled out the church register and discovered that he was really Gavriil, not Mikhail.

By that time, Mikhail-Gavriil had lived quite a long life and nothing should have surprised him. But something unexpected happened. Gavriil nearly went insane. He plucked at his beard the whole time and they found it almost impossible to calm him down. To be truthful before Almighty God, he was already a bit crazy, but nobody expected such a reaction from him. I mean, having the wrong name is a big deal; but even so.

Anyway, although he hadn't yet turned forty at the time he learned about his real name, Mikhail had already led an eventful life. If nothing else, he'd served in the First World War and as a very young man, he had been a sergeant major. At first, he was under the command of the Czar's officers, and after that he took orders from the Ministers of Defence in the provisional government, and after that, the Bolshevik Commissars. To cut a long story short, he was a soldier and a heroic one. He really was. He was awarded the St George Cross four times, in gold and silver, and in all four degrees of merit, as well as a medal for courage. You would think that would suffice? No one knows what he did to get these medals, he never told anyone, apart from how he was given the most recent one, a St George Cross, which was apparently awarded to him for finding the rest of his medals.

At that time, Mikhail was a spy, and when he returned to his dugout after one of his assignments, he discovered that somehow, on the way back, he'd lost his medals. It was an awful thing to happen but, as I described earlier, Mikhail could sometimes get fixated on unexpected things. That's what happened with the medals, but this time he did his best to put things right and returned to the enemy's quarters and recovered them. And for that particular action, he was awarded his fourth St George Cross. Then, apparently, after the war, some Ukrainian Cossacks near Smolensk managed to rob him of his possessions, all apart from his medals. Mikhail wouldn't part with them for anyone. He would rather lose his soul.

***

That night, Tantsia couldn't sleep and, in spite of the great plans she'd been making the previous evening, and the neatly packaged pies she'd baked, the next day she hesitated for a long time about whether or not to go to the waters. Her eyes were swollen. But, eventually, she set off.

She wished she had left earlier, in the morning. It was now terribly hot and she was breaking into a sweat. She hoped she wouldn't bump into him straight away. There were fewer people than usual at the upper spring, and she thought she'd have a chance to tidy herself up first.

As soon as she arrived at the waters though, she noticed the man from yesterday. Near the ash tree. He was sitting with his back towards her. 'I think he's eating. What a stroke of luck, he's alone. How tall he is!' He was sitting down but his height was obvious.

Suddenly Tantsia became nervous. Up to now, she'd never had any doubts about her looks. She knew there was no question that she was a gorgeous woman. How could anyone not like her? Now, though, she was uncertain. What if he didn't? She was so much shorter than him and if he stood up he might not see her, so Tantsia decided to seize her chance while he was still seated. She walked round in front of him, and before he could get up, she knelt and put the basket of pies down before him.

'Do you like it?' the man asked her.

'Aye,' Tantsia replied. 'Did you make it yourself?'

'Yeah,' said the man and he added something, but Tantsia couldn't make out what he'd said.

Embarrassed, she dragged the basket towards him. 'Eat!'

So that's how Mikhail and Tantsia got to know each other. At first they met one another every second day, as if by accident. They would meet at the springs. Mikhail would be working, bottling water and Tantsia would bring her pies. Mikhail began to give her presents, little things, like wooden spoons, or berries threaded on pieces of grass. As for Tantsia, she began making *khachapuris*, cheese pies, not to sell, but as a way of going to some trouble for Mikhail. She yearned for Mikhail to visit her so she could show him her beautiful house and serve him food, but was too shy to say so. Besides, he worked late and apparently he shared his accommodation with other foreign men. He started work at the crack of dawn so when would he have time?

But then, in the autumn, Mikhail did come to visit her at home, bringing another gift, this time mushrooms wrapped up in a shirt. No one else in the gorge would risk eating such mushrooms, but Tantsia wasn't afraid. She sat down on her sofa and watched Mikhail cook the mushrooms, and afterwards they ate them together, and then Mikhail stayed. That's how it transpired that a man came into Tantsia's life, and into her house.

There must have been a lot of gossip in the gorge. Of course they were gossiping, what would you expect? At first they gossiped, then they became jealous. Then they shut up. Tantsia wasn't bothered by any of it, she was happy. When the weather turned cold and the holidaymakers left, she didn't have to go to the waters either. She waited for her man at home. As for Mikhail, it's true he drank, but only up there with the men. He never showed himself to Tantsia when he was drunk. But it's also true that once, when he was drunk, he got into a vicious fight. He beat someone up and then was badly beaten himself. Nevertheless, he went to Tantsia, and she was pleased to see him, although it's hard to say why. It was that night Mikhail left his treasure, that's to say his medals, at her place, and Tantsia put them on the mantelpiece.

'My beauty,' Mikhail would say to her, stroking her hair. Tantsia would kiss his hand in response and with bated breath, try to make sense of his story.

She managed to understand some things, such as how, very early on, Mikhail had owned two horses, fast as bullets. They were known as New Bullet and Old Bullet, but the collective farm confiscated them from him. She also understood that, back then, when he lived a long way away, and of course, before Tantsia had met him, he had a wife and seven children. They died on their way to a labour camp. Mikhail then lived alone in a remote and awful place called Sheleska. He didn't have a woman there or anything, but since he could read and write, he was employed as a clerk in a local office. Mikhail told her these stories while stroking her hair, and Tantsia couldn't say anything in response. They couldn't really communicate.

Only once did they have something that might be called a conversation; it was when Mikhail entrusted her with the story about his name.

'Mikhail-Gavriil sounds a bit like Michael-Gabriel,' laughed Tantsia.

'Why are you laughing? They were archangels.'

'The appearance of those angels is a portent of death. As for me, when I was baptised, I was given the baptismal name of the daughter of the household: Margalita. Do you know that "margaliti" is Georgian for pearl?'

'So is your name really Margarita?'

'Yes, that's right, what of it?'

'Nothing. You have the same name as my house. It was called Margarita Stantsia.'

One evening Mikhail didn't appear. Tantsia thought he must have gotten drunk. It was a bitterly cold night and she felt sorry for her man. Who knows, perhaps he'd fallen asleep in the street. Mikhail had told her that once he'd slept out in a frost that was so cold, when he spat, his saliva froze solid in the air. Even so, Tantsia thought that tomorrow she would say to Mikhail, however drunk you may be, come to me anyway, not just because the weather's turned cold, but because there are wild beasts out there, and I don't want any harm to come to you. It took her quite a while to compose this little speech. Then, when she'd practiced it several times, she fell asleep.

Mikhail didn't appear the following day, nor the day after. When she went up to the springs, they informed her that Mikhail and the other men had been taken away. Taken away where? They shrugged their shoulders. Who knows?

To Sheleska! They must have taken him there! It's the most horrible place! Oh dear, Mikhail! And what about your medals? You've left your medals behind!

***

That summer, as usual, Lord Margalita arrived in the gorge. Her visits to her native area weren't inspired by any particular love of the place. It was just that the lady could afford to keep herself more easily in the village, and she was respected there. How could she, Margarita, the daughter of a lord, admit that she had to live in a communal apartment in town, and keep herself alive by teaching French? As you know, in summer, no one needs a teacher.

So, the lady arrived in the gorge.

Margarita was a particularly good example of her class and generation. She was snobbish and superficially educated. She thought she knew it all and that she was an expert in everything. She was rather religious too, and, certainly, she always took the moral high ground. She'd never been married, not because of her plain looks or general uselessness, but because of her circumstances. As a consequence, she viewed any relationship between a man and a woman with suspicion. She hated communists and peasants. She used to say, 'They don't know their cake from their coal.' And when she caught her brother's child hanging out with the plebs—that's to say the other kids from school—she went to great lengths to pay her sister-in-law a special visit, specifically to reprimand her, 'It's imperative to keep an eye on that child, Nina!' For some reason, she was very proud of this turn of phrase and often told people about her heroic deed.

You can imagine how a lady of such a disposition would react when she heard the news in the gorge that Tantsia, who had been brought up in the house of her parents, was pregnant by some Russian prisoner. Margarita was indignant and went straight to the house of this immoral and ungrateful woman to give her a good telling-off.

She liked the word 'ungrateful' very much, just as she was keen on the words she'd spoken to her sister-in-law. And the main accusation she levelled at Tantsia was precisely that: ingratitude. Why? Nobody knows.

But, to her great annoyance—and it really made her fume— Tantsia was in good spirits. She wasn't ashamed and she was so brazen that she was even making plans such as these:

'Until the baby grows up a little, I'll wait for Mikhail here. If he doesn't come, I'll go to Sheleska towards the end of winter. That's what I'll do! I don't know how, but I'll get there. He must be there, where else can he be?'

'Perhaps he's dead?'

Tantsia laughed. She thought, 'What nonsense!' but didn't say so out loud. Then she laughed again. Where else would he go if not back to his home, Margarita Stantsia?

But she didn't say that either, she just took the medals from the mantelpiece and showed them to the lady. 'He will come back, what else can he do?'

'Are they made of gold?'

'Of course they are.'

That was a good enough reason for him to come back.

That night the lady was dragged from her bed. 'Tantsia's giving birth,' they said, 'and she wants to see you, Lord Margalita.'

She hurried, but even so, it took a while to get dressed and to cross the water, and by the time she reached Tantsia's house, everything was over.

Tantsia wasn't young. In fact, she was approaching fifty. She was only three years younger than Margarita. And, as the lady was informed at the door, she had died in childbirth and entrusted her smiling soul, God knows to whom. Perhaps she was reunited with Mikhail, who knows?

Exactly three months later, people from the gorge accompanied Margarita to the station. The villagers carried gifts whilst the lady awkwardly clutched a baby girl against her chest. Tantsia had already been forgotten but the new baby had the same surname as the lady herself, and she had her first name too. This little girl, Tantsia's daughter, was called Rita, short for Margarita.

2.

In the old district, in a street which had had its name changed three times in the past forty years, in one of the rooms of a merchant's house, which had been converted into communal flats, there hung a rug. It was a rather beautiful rug, with the date '1910' embroidered in the corner. It looked small on the huge wall. Under the previous owners, apparently, it had been hanging from the ceiling and had even once covered the sofa. The room was very big. Even a table with a chair on top wasn't high enough for cleaning the chandeliers. Once a year, in order to perform that task, with the help of the owner, who lived next door, they would lug with great difficulty a very heavy folding ladder into the room. Margo would stand on the table and Margarita, sitting on the ladder, would pass down to her bits of the chandelier. Margo would tuck them against her chest, climb down to the chair and after that to the floor, where she would carefully put the magical objects—bronze flowers, glass balls—into a huge pitcher of soapy water.

The room had two high, narrow windows and Margo could easily sit on the window sills. She used to sit there and look at the house opposite with its archway. Margo was convinced that if she went through the arch, she would end up in a tunnel, and that tunnel would lead to the David Gareji monastery, where Margarita had once taken her. She'd seen a tunnel there.

Margarita took her out and about all the time. Margo was very happy to go on such excursions and however tired she may have been, she tried never to complain; she didn't want to disappoint Margarita and be left behind at home. It was nice at home too, though. If nothing else, she could listen to fairy tales on records, but only the ones where horrible things never happened: the one, for example, where the genie came out of a lamp; ones like that. But outings were better. And afterwards she would tell little Pavlick how she'd seen a lizard this big, no, this big, and she'd eaten a pie in Mtskheta, and many other things. But the problem was that Pavlick was also growing up and was no longer as friendly to Margo. He was ashamed of the fact that Margo was a girl, but that was only in front of other people. If Margo went to his place and nobody was around, they were still very good friends and they told each other thousands of secrets.

She even told Pavlick that the medals pinned to the rug were found by her grandfather in the war. Those medals were made of gold. She and Pavlick climbed onto the table, examined the medals from upclose, and even touched them. But all this happened in secret, because if Margarita ever found out, she would get very angry and would probably stop loving her.

According to Margo, these medals that her grandfather had found really were St George's Crosses. So it must be that St George had lost them and then her grandfather found them. Margo had even seen St George once. Pavlick didn't believe her, but never mind. She, Margo, knew for sure that when they were at the Shio-Mgvime Monastery, she'd definitely seen him that day. She wasn't mistaken at all. It was definitely St George.

Margo had been to Shio-Mgvime many times, as it was a regular haunt of Margarita's. They could get up there easily enough, as on the way some car would always stop to give them a lift. Coming down was difficult though, because men got drunk up there and returned late, and Margarita wouldn't ride in a drunken man's car.

That day too, it was a similar story. It was sweltering and Margarita and Margo became very tired, although they wouldn't show it. After a little while, Margo fell behind and as well as that, some stones got into her shoes and she couldn't push them out with her toes. So she sat down and began taking off her shoe.

'Hey, what's the matter, are you tired?' Margarita was ahead, waiting for her.

'No,' Margo answered, 'I've just got stones in my shoes.'

Margarita approached her.

'Come on, get up,' she told Margo. 'It's not much further. At the next bend, St George will meet us. He'll put us on his horse and give us a ride.'

St George didn't meet them at the bend. Probably, Margarita was mistaken about which bend it was; but he wasn't at the next one either, nor the next. Margarita had lied to her.

But what could be done? Once on the train, though, Margo could not help herself; she said to Margarita, 'You are a grown up woman, Margarita; lies don't suit you.'

'You silly thing,' answered Margarita. 'This train is pulled by St George's horse, didn't you know? Do you think it goes by itself? Think, who could cope with so many carriages?'

The train whistled, and suddenly the horse neighed! It really did! And as it went round a bend in the tracks, Margo saw with her own eyes that St George was at the front of the train! I swear, Pavlick! He was sitting on a big white horse, he had long hair and it was flaring it out in the wind. He was so handsome!

Pavlick didn't believe it. If she hadn't seen it for herself, Margo wouldn't have believed it either, but she had seen him and so what can you do?

But occasionally Pavlick was right when he didn't believe some things. Margo agreed to have her head shaved because she'd been told that instead of her red hair, it would grow back golden. Pavlick immediately said, they are lying to you, such things don't happen. And he was right. The red hair grew back again, and this time not curly but straight. Margo was very upset, but what could she do?

But Rita had black hair and blue eyes, and Margarita kept saying that our Rita was the most beautiful girl; she really was a beauty. And it's true, Rita really was beautiful. Once Margo spotted her at her school and called her name so that everybody could see what a beautiful mother she had, and everyone agreed that her mother was cool. Sometimes, secretly, away from Margarita and Pavlick, Margo would put black tights on top of her head, then she would toss her plaits behind her shoulders and wriggle her hips in front of the mirror. She'd do it carefully, because she was standing on the stool looking into the mirror of the dressing table. And in fact, with dark hair, she did look a bit like Rita. At night, when Margarita slept under the rug in an old bed, Margo would make a nest from the blanket on her sofa and she would grab her small toes with her hands and would dream. Margo thought, 'My mother Rita, you are the most, most beautiful woman. I love you so much, my mother, Rita!' Then she would start crying, only she didn't know why.

***

Margo didn't really remember all this very well. There wasn't that much to remember. Margalita didn't often take her out to the countryside these days, because she'd got old, and besides, Margo had to study: German, music and ballet. Then it was decided that she already knew enough German. Then she left music school because she played so badly and finally, the ballet teacher told them not to bother, the child isn't in the least artistic and the most she can hope for is the corps de ballet, and she's not really even up to that.

Be that as it may, Margo did find an occupation: she began fortune-telling. How she came up with that idea, no one knew. She didn't waste time on casting spells and such like, and because she was also young, she wasn't in a position to persuade even the most stupid woman that she could change her life by sheer dint of effort. She simply read fortunes in coffee grounds, for five roubles a time. If the client brought other women along, she'd give a discount and so on.

Everyone was happy: both those women who'd lost hope in

life and wanted to find out their destiny, and Margo. Even Margalita didn't complain. No one offered her money as such, but it was a relief: there was no problem affording food and, if she asked, Margo never refused to give her money. She would give precisely the sum of money the lady asked her for. But there was one thing: Margarita found it very difficult to ask Margo for anything. Margalita didn't love Margo and deep down, she was afraid of the red-haired girl.

All of a sudden, Rita, who had barely stayed for more than two days in their house as far back as Margo could remember, decided to return home. Margalita was happy, but as far as Margo's life went, it was the beginning of a period of constant arguments.

'What the hell does she want? Why is she coming back?' Margo asked Margalita. Rita was asleep and surprisingly for a woman of her appearance and build, she was snoring very loudly.

Margalita explained that she'd brought Rita up, that she was her girl and that's why the house was hers as well. And it was none of Margo's business. Was that clear? The lady was no good at arguing, but she was adept at upsetting people.

'Yeah, yeah, yeah, Margalita, Margalita.'

'What?'

'Nothing.'

It's true that at the beginning Rita didn't have it in for Margo, she just didn't consider her important. Nor was Margo terribly keen on socialising with her mother.

But, all of a sudden, maternal feelings arose in Rita, pure as a clear blue sky. She suddenly got the idea that, after leaving school, Margo should enter the university. Margo was rather surprised. What sort of idea was that? And whose idea was it? That idiot, illiterate whore Rita's of course! For nearly a month Margo listened to her attempts at persuasion, and then Margalita explained to Rita exactly what Margo was like. According to Margalita, Margo had some remarkable qualities; for example, as the Russians would say, she was a mentally and emotionally retarded cretin.

Of course, Margo did not consider herself to be retarded. On the contrary, she was convinced that she was a clever girl. But all this criticism was still irritating.

Margo consoled herself with the fact that people eventually get fed up with grumbling about the same topic, especially when that grumbling doesn't get them anywhere. For example, Margalita had been nagging her for many years. What do you think you look like? Why are you speaking like that, walking that way, breathing like that? But so what? If Margalita wasn't actually watching her, Margo would still put her elbows on the table.

When Pavlick was taken into the army, his mother, Seda, also had time on her hands. She wasn't really a bad woman, and wasn't hostile to Margo, but she decided to stick her oar in too with regard to the plans for Margo's future, even though Margo was already old enough to have her own passport. She introduced her to a smelly priest. The priest went to Seda's place every day and kept explaining to Margo that fortune-telling was sinful and any money earned that way would bring her misfortune.

Margo was well aware that the priest was Seda's lover. His pretending to be concerned for the state of somebody's soul was a way of pulling the wool over people's eyes. Seda always received one out of every five roubles of Margo's meagre earnings for acting as her secretary.

Well, what could she do? She couldn't hire Margalita as a secretary, could she? Seda had the advantage of always being at home.

For that reason, Margo didn't say a word. The priest kept visiting over and over again, until finally he got bored of eating Seda's jam and talking to Margo, and disappeared. Although Seda cried and was miserable, Margo was relieved. That priest was a real moron.

***

One evening, for some reason, Margo went to Mtatsminda, the pantheon on Tbilisi's Holy Mountain. Patriotism and national sentiment were totally alien to Margo, so she probably went there simply because the weather was nice. As Margalita said, Margo had a simple, peasant soul.

When Margo returned home she heard Rita's laughter in the corridor. 'She's got herself high, she thought.'

The three of them were standing near the communal lavatory: Rita, Margalita, and Seda. Rita was choking with laughter, Seda was roaring her head off, and Margalita was miserably silent.

Later, when Margo related the story, she'd say, 'The guardian angel whispered to me: leave it alone, don't get involved.' But at that time Margo's relationship with her guardian angel wasn't particularly good, so she didn't pay much attention to his advice.

It appeared that Margalita wanted to go to the lavatory but there was a huge rat in there. The lady was naturally frightened so she called Rita for help. Rita, of course, thought it was funny and was roaring with laughter. Seda was frightened of the rat too and so they were standing there like idiots.

'Look, Margo's here,' said Seda, for no particular reason. Rita was gasping for breath from laughing so much.

Margo took a laundry bowl full of clothes from the three-legged stool and glared at Rita. Rita stopped laughing. Later, during a big row, Rita shouted, 'Admit it, admit it! You wanted to hit me!' But at that point, standing there near the lavatory, in the corridor permanently illuminated by a dusty light bulb, the look in Margo's eyes, with their indeterminate colour, struck her as extremely evil and she retreated into a bitter silence.

Then Margo opened the lavatory door. There really was a rat sitting in the lavatory, and it was enormous and wet. Rita shrieked, and Margo threw the stool at the rat and hit it. While Rita carried on screaming and the rat was thrashing around, Margo went into the lavatory, grabbed the stool again, hit the rat once more and killed it. Rita stopped shrieking. Everybody was silent.

Margo straightened up. She was holding the bloodied stool in her hand.

'Throw it away,' Rita told her.

'What? Won't I need it anymore?' asked Margo.

'You were amazing!' Seda told her afterwards. 'It wasn't Rita who got frightened, it was me. As for Margalita, she was terrified. Rita told me later how our Margo turned out to be horrifying.'

'But wasn't the rat horrifying?'

'Yes, but you were even more horrifying.'

'Poor Seda, you don't know what "horrifying" means,' Margo thought.

'Okay, I'm on my way!'

Seda very much wanted to say something kind. She felt sorry for Margo too. Where could she go? But she couldn't think of anything so she said, 'Don't be offended by Margalita. Alright, she yelled at you. But so what? As if you never yelled.'

'Never. Or else I would have told Rita to fuck off thousands of times. Just remember that. Go well, Seda. When Pavlick comes back, say hello to him for me.'

'But you'll return before then.'

'I don't think so. Remember me kindly. So long!'

Seda didn't see her to the door, she remained sitting on the leatherette divan. Then, shuffling along in her slippers, she went to the window and looked across the street.

It was getting dark. Margo was nowhere to be seen. In front of the arch of the house opposite, three guys were standing and spitting through clenched teeth.

'Have you seen Margo?' Seda called to them in Russian.

One guy waved his hand, gesturing that she'd gone that way. 'Shall I go after her?' he asked.

'No,' Seda replied.

There was still shouting coming from Margalita's room. Oh, this Rita, what a voice she's got on her! Seda closed the curtain and went back to the divan.

3.

'What's this, the queen?'

This son of a bitch is so beautiful, Margo was thinking. Luckily, it's me who is leaving as I wouldn't be able to bear it if he abandoned me.

'You're a very handsome man. I expect all the women are crazy about you, aren't they?'

'You're a strange lady, Margo. Are you a bit soft in the head by any chance?'

'Don't get worked up, sweetheart, I simply said it for the sake of saying it. But you know, I never make any mistakes, I'm a witch!'

'What the hell is this? These shoes have so many laces,' Margo thought, 'why did I buy them?'

'Beautiful shoes.'

'But what can one do?' Margo thought. 'It's impossible to put them on or take them off.' At last she managed to tie the laces, and straightened up.

'Are you really leaving?' he asked.

'Yup!'

'Why do you keep saying "yup" to everything? What's wrong with you?' he asked.

'It's an Osho meditation technique. Keep saying "yup" and the world will say "yup" to you. Yup.' And then she thought, 'Yeah, sure, if not today, tomorrow.'

The man began mimicking Margo, saying, 'The man whose rib I was made of—me, Margarita—was particularly weak. He couldn't bear the pain. He could not give up his brilliant, stupid rib and succumbed to his grief, or something else happened to him.'

'Tell that to the birds!' Margo thought.

The man continued impersonating Margo: 'At least the guy with the rib doesn't exist anymore and I'm here, and I must be strong. And I am leaving!'

'Come on,' said Margo.

'I am leaving, but I don't want to go,' the man carried on impersonating her.

'Yeah, you're right,' Margo thought.

'I'm leaving this town which I love very much. I'm leaving because you're crushing me, and out on the road everything is clear. If I get fucked, I'll just shake it off, get up and walk away, but if I'm robbed, they'll pick me clean.'

'And then? You blabbering twit,' thought Margo.

'Out there on the road, I'll be spared women—wives who abandon you, the ones you are afraid to abandon, women you want, but you can't have. I'm going on the road, and there are no women there, and I'm not a woman, and no women, past or future, can touch me. So there, Margusha!'

'I'm off too. You go well.' Margo was playing his game. 'But I'll be back, just so that I have a reason to go away again. Stop fucking around. I'm off. Remember me kindly.'

As she went out of the door, she picked up a small stone, turned it the other way up and left. She was knowledgeable about 'stone stuff' and other such superstitions.

'I'll soon be in Tbilisi. One more journey, one more night, and it'll all be over.'

***

Margo liked apartments with high ceilings. She felt at home in old townhouses. She could quite easily live anywhere and could probably sleep peacefully in a luggage rack. But her love of apartments with high ceilings was of a different order.

Although Margo certainly had no awareness of the work of Dr Freud, she had to admit that her seemingly illogical reasons for loving apartments with high ceilings must have their roots in her childhood. On the other hand, why did she need to look for reasons? She found them, in the old house, in one of the rooms of the communal apartment, where a rug hung on the wall. In any other room, the rug would have reached the floor, but here it looked tiny, and the embroidered date '1910' was somewhere up towards the ceiling.

That probably explains why, on her way home, Margo was feeling pleased to be spending the last night in that apartment, although anyone else would be appalled by it. After groping her way through an entrance full of stinking cats and urine, she had to knock on the enormous door for ages until it was eventually opened by a strange woman. It was obvious she was still half-asleep. She didn't say hello, nor goodbye, and went back inside silently.

The room was airless. There was no air whatsoever, neither good nor bad. The windows must have been sealed to keep mosquitoes out, and the few shutters that remained were also closed. It was very hot. When her eyes got used to the darkness, Margo managed to make out that in the one room, there were women sleeping all over the place, a whole lot of women. They slept anywhere there was space: on the leatherette divan, above which a mirror was shimmering, on the table, and, most importantly, on the floor. They had their heads together, they were muttering and moaning, and no one heard the arrival of the newcomer.

But what a room! Six corners and a five-meter-high ceiling! Margo understood she'd got herself a decent place. She did not expect such a nice room from this gang of Hare Krishnas.

Somebody lifted her head and then went back to sleep. Sssshsh!

'I've gone mad,' somebody said.

'Some people are just hopeless,' Margo thought.

Margo, that is to say our Margarita, with her fiery red hair, was past 'a certain age' but could never be called feeble. Instead of becoming an alcoholic or going mad, she set up an excellent business together with two other cheats: she was a tarot card reader; they were an astrologer and a clairvoyant.

Obviously all three of them knew they were frauds, but they didn't admit it; as well as making fools of their clients, they wanted to fool each other, and surprisingly, they were pretty good at that. One Wednesday, the day of the week when, according to the rules, fortune telling was forbidden, the astrologer and clairvoyant decided to demonstrate their skills to Margo.

These two honorable experts began discussing Margo's personality without any tension between them. Margo didn't attempt to remember all the words of their blabbering. She only retained the idea that, apparently, some things had been happening to her for centuries. It seemed she was the way she was because of the seizure of land from the peasant farmers back in the 1930s, and the fact that she was under the influence of generations of 'Margaritas.'

'And so?' Margo asked them.

'And so, what?' The astrologer was indignant. She was standing in front of the mirror and tidying up her eyebrows. 'What do I look like? I don't want to see myself in the mirror.'

'Well, don't look then. I don't. And so?'

'Do you remember the mythical cow, Io? It gave birth to Heraclius.'

'Do you mean I'm Heraclius?' laughed Margo. 'Or the cow? What has that got to do with anything?'

'You fool,' said the astrologer. 'You will give birth to Heraclius. These legends exist for a reason.'

'How will he be conceived?' Margo was now sincerely interested.

'How do you think conception happens? With a finger? Don't be so stupid!'

Margo wouldn't have bothered to elicit this story and would not have returned, if she hadn't heard from the only person connecting her with home. Seda had informed her that Margo's mother, Rita, had been found dead on the tracks at Didube railway station. Seda had contacted Margo and told her in order to avoid calling Margalita, whose name Margo hadn't heard for eleven years.

'It's strange, but I feel sorry for her; somehow I'm touched,' Margo explained to her colleagues. 'To be honest, though, I really don't want to go there at all.'

That was the truth. Margo was happier being with people from foreign tribes. She could deal with all kinds of people from all walks of life, and in general, it was difficult to say who was, for her, actually a foreign tribe.

'I wish I understood which tribe I belong to,' Margo fretted. 'Darling Rita, to hell with her, may her soul have eternal light. But what happens now? She never gave me any clues about where I came from. Was it that she didn't know herself, or was it just her usual cruelty? And Margalitochka definitely doesn't know where I was dragged in from. She's pitiful. On the other hand, does it matter? I know exactly when I was born. It was the year when, according to my mother, lots of important things were going on in the West, but because of me, she was stuck, hanging around in Tbilisi. Anyway, she was a snake, that Rita. I'm sure she named me Margo out of spite. She wanted to infuriate Margalita by making sure one more defective would have her name and surname. Let a dog piss on her soul! Obviously, I mean on Rita's soul. I don't want to harm the poor old lady, she has her own troubles.'

4.

'When I used to get off the train, from the last carriage, I only had to run down the steps, cross the street and there was my house. I considered it mine, but now in that apartment there was nothing left that I owned. All my belongings had been stuffed in my handbag. The truth is, the house belonged to a strange man who spent the night there twice a week, in the big room. He paid the rent and he also paid the bills for the electricity and telephone. I was dying of shame.'

'Oh dear,' gasped Margalita. 'Did you use his money to call me!?'

'Yeah, what else could I do?'

'It was so nice that you phoned!'

'Yes, I was happy too.' And Margo thought, 'It was the least I could do, to phone someone.'

'Then what happened?'

Poor Margalita! How miserable your life must have become that you're glad to see me!

'On the days when he was due to come, I rushed around cooking him three different dishes, but that didn't work either. He would invite me to a restaurant and cover the prices on the menu with his hand. I was never able to pay my way so he would respect me.'

'He must have been a nice man though, wasn't he?'

'He was cool. The apartment was cool too, with high ceilings. The cornices were decorated with some kind of bas-relief shit. From the window, you could see the station and from five in the morning there was this woman's unpleasant voice shouting out station announcements.'

'Did it wake you up?'

Margo was sitting on Margalita's bed and thinking, 'How amazing, I think she cares about me.'

'No, it didn't bother me at all. It was only on the first night I dreamed that I was at Sukhumi station and the Tbilisi train was being announced. Anyway, I prefer it when there's the sound of somebody yelling in the street, at least that way I know I'm alive.'

'I'm alive' was a good feeling. Margo especially felt it when the train travelled the narrow passage between the two museums, with the deaf walls and the train pounding. Every morning she would look up at the ceiling and shout, 'My God, how wonderful!' Now, it gave her no pleasure to remember these words. It's been a long time since she woke up with these words in her head. She probably won't wake up with them again for a long time to come, not while Margalita is alive.

'Poor Margalita,' Margo was thinking, 'how could God do this to you, leaving you alone with me?'

'What happened then?'

'Then. Then I exercised every morning. I lay on my back trying to make circles in the air with my legs, writing my full name and surname and looking at that silly bas-relief. After that, I drank coffee in a civilised manner.

'In general, I did live in a very civilised manner. I was specially kitted out for it. I had a journalist's notebook and student identity card, although it's true it had someone else's name on it.'

'But what if someone had caught you?'

'No, man, why would they have caught me? I wandered around the whole town and the suburbs, I went to all the exhibitions, all the museums. I also went to a concert by a flute player from Damask, somewhere near Land's End. I didn't spend a penny, I had time on my hands, what did I care?'

Margalita listened to her. 'How tiny she is,' Margo thought. What a rotten fate destiny dished out to her. She's never had any man, nor any joy. At first Rita made her life a misery, then she rushed off and died, and now this pitiful woman was sitting displaying her photograph. Margalita saw that Margo was looking at the shelf and misinterpreted her gaze.

'Your mother was a beautiful woman.'

'Beautiful and a snake,' thought Margo and said, 'Beautiful.'

'Yes, I remember at school they were always telling me, "Your mother looks like the Italian actress Ornella Muti." Once they even saw her. She wore cool jeans too, Levi's or something.'

Margalita shrank completely into herself.

'She was a beautiful woman. I don't look like her, do I? It's a pity. I wonder who I do look like? Anyway, Margalita, if I had been butchered, would you display my picture? It's obvious, if I didn't phone, you wouldn't start looking for me. You'd be relieved. Fewer people, fewer problems.'

'I feel so sorry for her.'

'Don't make me cry! "So sorry"—what are you saying? Are you wondering why they killed her? Is that it?'

'Don't be angry with me.'

Margalita began to cry. 'What do I want from her?' Margo wondered. 'And, more to the point, what do I want from anyone?'

'Hey, Margalita, shall I tell you, or don't you want to know?'

'I do want to know.'

'So,' Margo thought, and laughed. 'That's exactly why Margalita is afraid of me. And Rita hated me for it. She thought I was accumulating resentment so I could do something to her later. What could I do?'

'Well, there was this place there, where at least three times a week I went to the restaurant. I liked it a lot. When I entered, the owner would shout at the top of his voice, "What a beauty has arrived! You aren't a woman, you are the sun!" I know it was a lie, but it lifted my spirits.'

'But, why?'

'Be quiet. So, I flirted with the barman too, and he really was the sun. A prince. You could say he was no intellectual, but who cares? As if intellectual men were ever of any use to me. This boy like a sun was adorned with thousands of silly tattoos, he had black hair and eyes. He was part Moroccan, and when he smiled at me, my heart stopped. If God was angry with me, or I made a mistake, such as not smiling at him when I entered, or if I first greeted someone else, he would start clicking his fingers. "Excuse me a moment," he would say to the customer, and then he would come up to me and ask indignantly, "What's up?" It was false indignation because his eyes shone, showing that he knew exactly what the matter was. Even now, I don't understand why he liked me. All I needed was a scythe and I'd look like death personified! Once, while saying goodbye, he said to me, "Would you like me to give you a bunch of keys? You can put them in your pocket so the wind won't blow you away." He had a peculiar sense of humour, bless him.

'When I first stayed with him—it wasn't because of any huge passion, but more because I felt too lazy to drag myself onto the bus late at night—he put on a CD. Do you know what it was? Rain. It was a recording of real rain, with a thunderstorm and sounds of wind blowing. I was genuinely surprised that he'd thought of doing that, but it was good.

'So, when I fell asleep, I dreamed that I was in Birtvisi, I was sitting in the cave, in my yellow sleeping bag, and I felt great. Then I heard a voice:

'"Tuck your legs in further or you'll get wet." Do you know whose voice it was? Yours!' And then thought Margo to herself, 'Why did I come out with that?'

'Are you telling me the truth?'

'Yes. I hadn't heard your voice for years but how could I be mistaken? "Hey, Margalita," I said and woke up.'

Margalita looked radiant as she watched her. 'So be it,' thought Margo.

'And then?'

'And then, I'm telling you—I woke up. I was sorry it was only a dream but even so I felt very good.'

'Did you tell that man about it?'

'Yeah, I'd already told him that I had a granny called Margalita in Tbilisi.'

So, be happy.

'Why didn't you bring him with you?'

What's happened to you, Margalita, that you are asking such questions?

'Dunno. I left. I spent several months there feeling at home, but somehow eventually I realised it had turned cold. When I heard about Rita, it was a freezing night and I went to some bar. I sat in that bar, and after the beer had made me feel frozen rigid, I wandered home, and thought perhaps it was time to return to my homeland. So, I thought that, as I had nothing important to keep me there, I'd phone you, and here I am.'

'That's good.'

'Yes, it is good.'

***

Night fell. Margalita was sleeping under the rug in the old bed. She was very small, and her breathing was inaudible so it was impossible to tell whether she was breathing or not.

Margalita simply thought that the woman Margo had come to see her. But in fact there were two versions of Margo there: the visible one and, inside her, a little girl. Margo knew for certain that it was a little girl. She wasn't an expert fortune teller for nothing.

'Her father was so silly,' Margo thought. He kept saying they spent their time unwisely! How could they spend it more wisely?

'Poor you,' Margo whispered to the little one, 'How long have you been hiding? Perhaps you thought that this crazy person would rush to me and kill me? You're a silly girl. We went on such a long journey, and soon we will have such a surname! The same surname as the lady.'

Poor Margalita always used to say, 'We received retribution for our sins because we sold our motherland. If it wasn't for the revolution, Tantsia, Rita and you, Margo, would never have inherited our noble surname.'

'Well, fuck you!' Margo looked at the sleeping Margalita. 'As if you could ever have anything better than my unborn child!'

Now, how much time was left? One, two or five months? Not even that. Margo put her hands on her abdomen.

'The most important thing is that you shouldn't be sad. When Margalita dies and you grow up, I will sell the rug, put you in a rucksack, along with Grandpa's medals, and I'll definitely find that house of ours. Why should it be a problem to find a simple Margarita Stantsia?'

A FOREIGN MAN

Do you like my elephants? I'm very fond of them. Max gave them to me as a present. Oh, it's good that I remembered that. Do you recall how you once asked me whom I had loved? You set me the task of telling the story of a man and a woman. I'll tell you the story of Max. He was a very good man, but why do I say 'was'? He still is.

I have said before that I hate the month of November more than anything. November is vile just as it is, and not only that, winter follows soon after. To be blunt, if I die in November, it wouldn't bother me. I'm not intending to die just yet, but even so. To come to the point, if I died in November, I couldn't care less. As far back as I can remember, I've dreamed of loving some man during winter, so that not everything comes to an end in November. Up to now, I've never had such a love. At the end of autumn, either I run away somewhere to spend winter there, or else the man does the same. Any relationship I've started in November has never ended kindly. As someone once said, November snow is really a can of worms. And they were right. You wait and see, once November comes, disasters aren't far behind.

That guy Max came into my life precisely in November. Manana, Malashevskaya and I were sitting in the kitchen, waiting for Gurami to come along bringing beer and my new tenant Max. I knew that Max was old, a famous artist, that he would pay me well and would leave after ten days. The others couldn't care less about him. Back then, Gurami used to flirt with Malashevskaya, telling tales of his heroic deeds, Malashevskaya would strum the guitar and sing her heart out, and as for Mananiko, she would be completely drunk. She was in that state now and kept asking where

Gurami and the beer had got to.

Soon Gurami arrived, bringing the beer and Max too. Max wasn't old at all, he was exactly the age men usually are when I'm irresistibly attractive to them. If a man of this age happens to be fat, rich and a German speaker, he will tremble with love for me. No other beauty can possibly compete with me. I've experienced this often enough to recognise the situation precisely. I don't understand the reason for such a kindly disposition towards me, but it's proved to be useful. I've made the most of it many times. These angelic sugar daddies want nothing from me but my happiness.

Only Max, unlike my usual venerable admirers, wasn't fat. 'Sweet guy,' Mananiko announced. She was right.

That evening Max refused to go to bed. He drank beer and looked at me very attentively. He had grey eyes and he wore grey clothes too. The stupid gear I wear now, winter and summer, is Max's style, only back then I hadn't torn holes in the armpits.

Since he was watching me so shamelessly, I stared shamelessly back at him. He became very cheerful, asking, 'Are you bewitching me, my little babe?' 'What if I am?' I retorted. These terms of endearment stayed with me to the end, although you could not say that I was little then, and it's unlikely I was a witch either.

When the beer was finished, Malashevskaya shoved Manana and Gurami into the car and drove them away. When I returned I discovered Max was doing the washing up. 'What are you doing?' I said. 'Nothing,' he replied.

Damn me! While Max was cleaning the kitchen, I went out and bought a bottle of moonshine for a rip-off price.

That night I discovered that, before he went grey, Max had red hair, that he had a wife and two kids, and that he hated fresh tomatoes and cheese. He found out that I was nineteen years younger than him, that I had been brought up by a German, and that I couldn't sleep in winter. By dawn, we'd established that it was very good that Max had come and would be living at my place, and then we went our separate ways because he had to go to the gallery early.

In the morning, Max was already waiting for me in the kitchen. He had just come out of the bathroom and he covered his chest with his hands in a very funny way, like Mr Pitkin in the films.

I dragged myself along to the exhibition opening and thought proudly what a good artist he appeared to be. I don't know why I was proud. Max greeted me as if he'd been waiting for me his entire life. 'Do you like my paintings?' 'Very much,' I said. 'Especially these elephants.' He laughed and told me that the elephants were magic. When happiness comes, the third elephant will turn in our direction.

After that we were together all the time. In the afternoon we wandered around the town, buying thousands of silly things in the market. Sometimes we were invited to parties. And at night, we sat in the kitchen and chatted. Max told me stories of 1968. Once he told me how he and his wife and children had been arrested in Bulgaria because his wife took her top off and painted suns on her breasts. We talked incessantly and only stopped when Max would say, 'I'm an older man so you must take notice of me. It's time to sleep.'

On the eve of Mananiko's birthday, on the pretext of asking me to help organise things, but in reality hoping that I would have money and food, Gurami and Malashevskaya arrived. Misha followed them. They had bumped into him in the street and brought him along.

Misha had a very precise function in my life, just as I had a precise function in his. He was an unusual guy, much younger than me, and noticeably handsome. As for me, I was over the hill, with crooked legs and back problems, and looks were nothing to brag about.

We spent two years together. The truth is, during this time he never offered me a kind word nor any presents. He was a cheerful guy, with no hang-ups, and neither of us had any expectations of the other. Any port in a storm! To put it in a nutshell, we didn't love each other, and when he fell asleep I used to go to the kitchen and cry. Hopefully, Misha didn't cry. What reason could a man of that age have for crying?

Misha was somewhat put out by Max's existence. He didn't stay the night and he left with Malashevskaya and Gurami. 'If he were to see me in the morning I would die of embarrassment,' he said.

'Why did he leave?' Max asked me. I told him. Max was amused. Well, I know that Max was in up to his neck in the sexual revolution, but how could Misha be expected to know about that?

Max looked at me, then he filled up our glasses and asked me if I was in love with that boy. It was my turn to be amused. 'Maxy, darling, what are you inventing?'

We decided that night that we would go to Cuba, but before that we would go to Mananiko's birthday party. Since I'd need to know for the birthday party, Max taught me how to dance. 'Cha-cha—cha,' Max whistled. I tried to sing, 'One, two, three, cha-cha-cha. Was that right or wasn't it?' 'That's great,' Max said, 'Very good.'

When we were in the mountain village of Kiketi. Max gave Manana a huge bouquet and made such a huge bonfire that the flames reached the sky. It was November but we were sitting in t-shirts. Mananiko drank from the bottle and screamed to the sky, 'Hurray!'

'Wasn't I lovely when I had my hair down to my shoulders?' Malashevskaya sang as Gurami snuggled up to her, and her hair was down on her shoulders, and she looked lovely too.

On the way back, when we were squeezing ourselves into Malashevskaya's car, Max did something that made even me, someone who'd been a bohemian, a flower child, who'd lived in communes at various times in the past, nearly cry. He put his hand on my shoulders and kissed my back.

'Your name is written on the fence,' Shevchuk was singing.

'I love this woman!' Gurami was roaring in Russian, hanging halfway out of the car window. 'Hey, people, I love this woman!'

I was a coward, and when we went to the kitchen and Max put bottles out on the table, I asked him, 'Max, if I leave you alone tonight, would you find it a drag?' I said I would come in the morning and see him off. He laughed. 'What can I say?' he asked.

So I, an idiot and a coward, left. I went to Malashevskaya's place. She and Gurami weren't at all happy to see me. I lay down on the veranda and felt very ashamed, very cold and very sorry for myself. Then I couldn't bear it anymore and went home.

There was a light on in the kitchen. Max was sitting at the table. 'If you aren't that keen on going to sleep, let's drink,' he said.

Max told me that somewhere in Australia there live certain kinds of people. When the men from this nation go from one village to another, before reaching the village they sit on a stone and wait there a long time until their souls catch up with them.

'Just imagine,' said Max, 'how long I will be without a soul! Before my soul gets here from Tbilisi.'

The following day Max went away, leaving me these elephants. When happiness comes, the third elephant will also turn to face us. To tell the truth, I thought it would turn when you appeared. As you see, it didn't. Never mind.

Now, it's your turn to tell me something.

IT'S RAINING

'Has it been raining for a long time?' a tourist asks the boy who is splashing around in the puddles.

'I don't know, uncle,' replies the boy, 'I'm only seven years old.'

1.

I'm looking at probably the hundredth river in a row. But it's still beautiful. When I was crossing the bridge, down in the park, I noticed a waterfall. It reminded me of Poseidon and all that. Even though it was raining, it roared with full force and I thought I'd sit down nearby before going to the cinema. Yes, it had been raining, but I had a rucksack with me and I could have sat on that.

But I didn't have a chance to enjoy it. There was a couple near the waterfall, a fair-haired woman who looked like a man, and a gentle boy. They were kissing each other so passionately that I didn't dare to pass them. Well, big deal, you might say, but I didn't want to embarrass them. On the other hand, what a nice thing to see. In my town no one kisses each other, apart from drunken men. It seems that nobody loves each other.

So, seeing as I couldn't sit down at the waterfall, I followed the bank of the river. Then I felt lazy and sat down near the railings. I can see the church clock from here so I won't be late. So, I'm standing there and looking down into the water. The paved path is wet, and lying scattered along it are green leaves and some kind of soft, pink flowers, fallen from the trees. The river is green, just like this wet alleyway and so is the huge cathedral dome, only that's a different kind of green. The sun has already gone down. It will get dark soon.

It's raining again. It's drizzling and bearable. I'm standing there in a green alleyway that someone's been tending, on the bank of the river. Two ducks have paddled towards me. They are very cute, but I haven't got any food to give them. They turn tail immediately.

Those two people were kissing every time I looked in the direction of the waterfall. You people, it's raining! Some people have such a nerve!

And then what?

'Well, Dad, keep going. Can't you see it's been raining?' I smiled at him. 'It's a beautiful view.'

He smiled back at me too. He's got false teeth, of course. At his age, he couldn't possibly have grown new teeth. He's got feathers stuck in his hat, probably duck feathers.

All alone, all alone.

I became angry. Daddy, where were you in 1943? But then I couldn't be bothered to speak. I'm an idiot, what did Daddy have to do with all that? That's why I grinned again and asked him, 'What then?'

'Nothing.' He was offended, even so. 'I hope you have a nice evening.'

'Thank you.'

There was one man, I don't know what to call him—you couldn't say he was a lover or a boyfriend—he was just a good man. He used to say, *'All the way home, all the way home,'* and after that he would cast a meaningful glance at me and would add by way of explanation, 'Novalice.' That's the name of an author of fan fiction.

I knew that, so why say it? Here I am, looking at the hundredth river in a row, killing time before going to the cinema, getting rained on, and feeling angry with some daddy, who has silly feathers stuck in his hat and is going on his own way.

Hopefully, he's going to the old people's home. That's where he belongs.

2.

Madame Maria and I are sitting on the veranda, helping ourselves to coffee. Mme Maria, even now, is a most beautiful woman. She looks like Greta Garbo and she dresses accordingly. I love her very much, and she often says that she loves me too.

The tablecloth, laid out in the garden for breakfast, has a floral pattern. There's a tiny vase of flowers standing on the table. I don't know how, but I know the name of these flowers. They are primroses. Everything is delicious apart from the incredibly watery coffee. Mme Maria cares about health, mine and her own.

Health issues are one of her particular interests. On the whole, she's interested in two issues: health, as mentioned above, and the relationship between mankind and God. Some time ago, Mme Maria discovered the existence of God, and ever since, the Creator hasn't left her alone. She is always on the move, going to church, listening to preachers.

Now she's telling me what she was told by a fat priest. Apparently she'd intended to share this story with me straight away yesterday, but I was rather late coming home. This coming home late was very bad, because it's imperative to sleep for at least eight hours, especially if I want to live to Mme Maria's age. And of course I want to. Why wouldn't I?

Mme Maria is spreading honey on a bread roll. She's doing so very precisely, very neatly. She has a huge, blue sapphire ring shining on her finger, disfigured from polyarthritis.

She told me herself that she had polyarthritis, otherwise I wouldn't have known because I thought that everyone of her age had disfigured joints.

As for her eyes, they are blue and forbearing. She looks at me all the time, never takes her eyes off me. She's looking at me now. Even though she's spreading some honey on a roll, she's looking at me, but I'm not irritated. She's got nice eyes.

She sneakily licks her lips. She's intending to say something. Go on, Mme Maria!

'Listen!'

'I am listening, Madame Maria.'

'Were you with a man yesterday?'

Well, I am surprised. I'm nodding my head at her and smiling. I probably resemble a silly China man.

She puts down her knife in a business-like manner.

'Is he one of your kind?'

'No, Madame Maria.' I am smiling at her. 'He's from your social class.'

'That's a shame,' she says, biting on a roll. She chews it thoroughly. 'Once I had a man who was one of your lot. Yes, it was after the war. Six of them were billeted at my place. One was from your class. He used to fetch water. He was a nice guy. My God, how he fucked me!'

She really said that word, I swear it!

'Yes, fucked me.' She is looking at me with her bright blue eyes.

'What did you think? Everyone was fucking me.'

Mme Maria is chewing the bread roll and smiling at me. Is she mad?

'Yes, my dear girl, they were fucking me!' Suddenly, she performs that horrible gesture.

That's it. I think I'm going crazy with astonishment.

'Yes, yes,' chuckles Mme Maria and she demonstrates to me what they did to her, over and over again.

There's some kind of sweet, overpowering fragrance in the garden. It reminds me of the veranda of the Kuprelis in the Chugureti area of Tbilisi. The same bush, with its mauve and white flowers bloomed there too. I wasn't allowed to pick them, so I stood on tiptoe and stuck my nose in the bush.

'I'm off, Madame Maria. I'll be back on time today. Thank

you very much for breakfast.'

'Thank the Lord you enjoyed it.' She is nodding at me.

'Goodbye.' I smile at her and extend my hand.

'Listen.'

'Yes?'

'There's a blue umbrella in the doorway. Take it. It will suit you better.'

'Thank you, Mme Maria.'

Yes, yes ... I wonder which part of my body this umbrella will particularly suit?

3.

If Marta had been around, I wouldn't have allowed it to happen. She would have instantly shown me that only crazy people develop the habit of a one-way love. Marta was a cool girl. I never had such a precious companion as her. She was easy-going, straight forward, knew her own mind and didn't interfere with others. She didn't irritate me and nor did I get on her nerves. We used to meet at Toma's place, where Toma, as a rule, would prepare a salad for her husband, so that, God save us, the husband wouldn't lack vitamins. As for us, we would sit on the balcony and philosophize. Marta would immediately go on the attack.

'What is happening in your love life? What's your favourite boy doing? What's new?' It was refreshing to see Marta in Toma's house, where everything revolved around Toma's husband and housekeeping.

'I'm really interested in your life because Toma drives me crazy. Why doesn't she do anything I tell her? Whatever I suggest, she always says she has no money. She has a salary and no child, so I can't understand why she's incapable of spending money on herself.'

'I dunno, she's a silly girl.'

It was very hot. Oh, I wished it would rain. Rain, come on! We were gulping brandy we'd nicked from Toma's husband's desk. It was a Hennessy, but who cared about Hennessy? Tall Marta, in her red bra, was sitting on the rolled-up sleeping bag and was smoking some kind of shit. She had a crooked index finger on her right hand, there from birth, but it didn't make her ugly, in fact, the opposite. If it were straight, Marta would not be Marta. It was just that that the slim cigarette meant that her crooked finger caught my eye. I remember I asked her, 'Listen, does that menthol one make you cool?'

'No, and nor does that shit shampoo make you cool.'

'What shampoo?'

'The one with menthol. I saw an ad. It said it cooled you down, so I foolishly bought some and felt like a real fuckwit. That woman Toma told me that she had maternal feelings towards her guy Makhuna. Come on, get real! Is it normal to have motherly feelings towards a man?'

I was taken aback and I answered, 'Come on though, how is it I can have maternal feelings when a man's fucking me, then?'

'That's all due to Oedipus.' Marta was anxious. 'Don't you understand anything? This one, Toma, told me she had such feelings. I swear she's not lying. Can't you see how much she fusses around her husband? Haven't you noticed that if she pours some coffee for you, she first sips it from the spoon? Wow! That's because she does the same for that husband of hers. She pours the coffee, adds some sugar, stirs it, lets it cool down a bit and after that, wow, how nice it is! Now, one sip for mommy, and a puff of the cigarette for daddy!'

'I wish I could see them having sex. I wonder what kind of misery they inflict on each other.'

'She's probably a virgin!'

'What nasty things are you saying?'

'Toma forces me to be nasty by her bullshitting. I'm driven completely mad. She lacks only one thing. Her eyes should have been blue to please her husband. Trust this old cheat, when you get married don't start bullshitting. I'm not talking about washing, ironing, dinners, and so on, but as soon as you put sugar in the coffee, stir it, taste it to check it isn't too hot, and take it mincing along to his computer, and don't forget to call him "my genius," then he'll start cursing immediately and will get himself a lover. He'll consider himself to be very cool.'

Marta never simpered at her first husband, nor did she stir his coffee, and he left her. He ran off with a woman who did simper. She always called him 'my life' and 'my rose.' Marta changed her tactics with her second husband and took coffee not only to his computer at home, but virtually to his office in town. But what can one say? I didn't remind her about it, but she looked at me in such a manner that it was clear she understood it herself. I felt sorry for her.

I'm cool too when it comes to theory, but does that help?

A week after that conversation, we were supposed to go to Greece. We postponed the trip, hoping to persuade Toma to come with us. But this is what happened. That very night, Marta drove into a wall at a speed of a hundred miles an hour. It was raining heavily and they said later that her headlights weren't working and she hit the wall without even braking.

'She always drank too much. She was a piss-head,' declared Toma's husband. Toma immediately agreed with her husband and it felt like she was putting another nail in the coffin.

'So there we are.'

After that, I hated them both. I can't stand other women like Toma either.

4.

I remembered her for some reason, I don't know why she popped into my head.

She was a prostitute. We lived in the same hotel for a week, she was working, and I was living life to the full. She told stories, each one more incredible than the last, in a composed, calm way. Prostrate on the bed, she smoked and dropped ash on her breasts, which were covered in burns. At first I thought she'd had encounters with maniac clients, but there you go, how silly I was, there was a reason for burned breasts.

She told her stories to one and all. I found them entertaining. Rina lay around on the bed, I sat on the sill of the open window, and Rina recounted and recounted. The noise of the port came through the window, sometimes the muezzin called, sometimes I heard *Praise the Lord* and sometimes it sounded like *Halleluiah*, and meanwhile Rina gave voice to all her opinions with a long, incredible story, and she did it in such a reassuring way that I couldn't object. Anyway, she was right, and I was right too.

'What do you understand of men? Listen, there was this girl from Leningrad, from Peter-Petera; Irochka, that's what she called herself. I met her in Sukhumi on the Black Sea. Well, I met her and I was working and she was having fun. Her looks? I dunno, I don't like such worn-out women.

'Irochka's father was a professor, of what, how the hell should I know? Don't ask me, I don't know. She told me: something like ethno-something-something. I haven't a clue.

'Irochka was dressed fashionably for that era. She didn't work as a prostitute for the sake of clothes, she always had money.

'So, one day, near the coast, a local bloke met her in a coffee shop. I haven't a clue whether he was Abkhazian or Georgian. He had a long nail on his little finger, hairy, a gold ring, khaki colour trousers, nylon socks. You get the picture, don't you? He thought he'd reeled in Irochka, no trouble at all. Irochka thought the opposite.

'The following day Irochka told me that they'd been in some kind of hut on the opposite coast and she said that he was an incredible man. I believed her. She was definitely an expert on men, and besides, she had a brain. So, this Irochka decides to show her gratitude by going down on him. But, you won't believe this, that Georgian or Abkhazian guy said, "No, my girl, I won't insult you." Can you believe it?

'Anyway, Irochka went on her way, and some time later, with a good suntan and all the rest, she planned to return home. But before she did, she strolled into the town and suddenly somebody was calling her, "Irochka!" It was that Georgian or Abkhazian, I don't know, anyway, the guy from Sukhumi.

'He had a white car and black sunglasses, you get the picture, don't you? He wound down the window, took off his sunglasses and beckoned Ira with his finger. "Come here! How are you Ira?" he asked. Irochka answered, "Fine." "What? Have you been having fun?" he asked. Irochka said, "Yes." So that cowboy pulled up the car window, like in the movies, and Irochka's head got stuck. Irochka started giggling, "Let me go, you naughty boy." The guy told her, "So you've had fun, you whore." Irochka told him, "Let me go you bastard." So, it was a totally stupid situation, wasn't it?

'So, this golden guy got out of the car, approached our Ira from behind and had his way, and, what can I say? It's a crazy story.

'Obviously, he let her go afterwards. So, Irochka didn't fly out that day, nor the following day, and after that she introduced this Georgian or Abkhazian or whatever to her professor father in Leningrad, pardon me, Petersburg, with his fingernail, ring, and hair, and what-not. How do you like that? Then she married him. Can you imagine how he'd use her? Anyway, he beat her badly. I know it for sure. He definitely beat her up because of her past. But Irochka put up with it, tolerated it, or maybe she enjoyed it,

I don't know.

'Then this Georgian or Abkhazian, or whatever the hell he was, went for Irochka's mother too. No, I don't mean he beat the mother. That woman was pretty flattered. Can you imagine what it was like with her goat of a professor husband and then this one, Ira's Abkhazian? After that, he moved on to Irochka's sister, so Irochka became jealous and phoned the police.

'Anyway, they separated. Where they all are now, I don't know. And you tell me that Georgian men are useless? Okay, let this one be Abkhazian.'

So, that's the sort of woman Rina was, Rina or Shirina, I don't know, anyway, whatever she was called, she didn't show me her passport. But she was a real weirdo. A week later in the town where we were, one of the prostitutes had a baby, and Rina adopted him. I don't know why she wanted to do that. She felt sorry for him. 'He'll die in the orphanage,' she said, and she bribed somebody. Or perhaps not, I don't know that for sure. But that day, she brought him to the room and showed me the child. I had never seen a child of that size, absolutely tiny, dark and pitiful.

'I've called him "Beast." That was my late father's name.' She was once again lying prostrate on my bed. You're not supposed to smoke in the presence of a child and you can't open the windows when it's raining. She drove me mad with this little whore's son. She made me freeze and filled my bed with cigarette ash. 'Shirina was my mother's name and it's my name too, but it is not to be uttered by those bastards. Let them call me Rina and that's that.

'Only one called me Shirina, he was a very nice guy. At that time, I lived like a nun for one and a half years. He was cool. I wasn't young. I'm telling you a new story. How did I meet him? I was introduced to a guy in one of the clubs, and he was so good-looking that I fell over as if I'd been hit. He was the most handsome guy. But it wasn't just that. All my life I've attracted handsome men. You find that hard to imagine, don't you? That's how it was, a handsome man wasn't out of the ordinary for me. But, to put it simply, this one was special. How can I explain it to you? He was very noble. Why are you laughing? It's true. We didn't speak to each other directly, a man introduced us, and then this handsome guy invited me for coffee, and that was that. Because of him, I led the life of a nun.

'I didn't think about him for aeons. We phoned each other on some pretext a couple of times, and that was that. I was all alone but I was fine. I couldn't care less whether I was alone or not. I loved that guy. I loved him like a virgin. I thought, I'm too old for sex, but if I ever really need it, no one's refused me yet. I'll carry on for five more years I thought, and after that I won't even want it anymore.

'I sometimes bumped into that guy, but I'm telling you, nothing happened. And then, and this was amazing, something remarkable did happen. I was at home with mayonnaise on my head. Did you know, it makes your hair really soft? And while my mayonnaise was drying on my hair, I scoured my entire face to get rid of pimples and what-not. I did hara-kiri to myself. So, I'm sitting like that with my face all swollen, mayonnaise on my head and the telephone starts ringing. It's that guy. He invited me to a classical jazz concert. I told him, "No, thank you." I could certainly have washed my hair, but what could I possibly do with my face?

'Then, when my face was back to normal, in other words, the following evening, I called him and we went to hear the jazz that evening. The concert was on that day too. I hate jazz.

'Then, something hellish happened to me, doesn't matter what, and he kissed my poorly little finger that had been bitten, injured or bruised, I don't recall what kind of injury, but anyway, he kissed me. Then I cried for the whole night. He just blew my mind, that handsome guy.

'Yes, I don't know, we were friends for a long time but he

wasn't what I'd call a lover. I know very well what a lover is. And then what? Nothing, it was over.

'Fucking hell! Why are you bawling? I'm coming!

'But anyway, I wish it hadn't ended. But it was no big deal, instead of a great love I ended up having lots of sex again. So, at one stage I wanted to become a ballerina and here we are. Everything happens as it should. And what's a ballerina in love at the end of the day? An idiot.

'Yes, I'm coming! He was premature, born at seven months, the fucker ...'

I remembered Rina-Shirina very clearly. Anyway, I behaved like a cow. She gave me her number, but I never called her. I wonder what kind of man that dark Beast grew into.

5.

This is where I live. I will always live here from now on. It rains here all the time. They say it has always rained here and it will always rain. At the beginning I suffered, but now I know that rain's very healthy stuff. Here we are, my skin is clear too, it's the same as all the local women have. My nice skin isn't just due to the rain. I don't smoke anymore. Because it rains all the time here, everything is damp and cigarettes taste bad. I don't drink any more either, because it's expensive and also because if my boss found out, he would fire me. That's why my complexion is so clear and I am very pale, like the walls in my flat. The walls in my flat are absolutely white, like the ones where I work. In the beginning, I thought I would put up some pictures, but then it was raining so I changed my mind about going out to buy them. In any case, I walk a lot, to work in the morning, from work to the cafeteria, from the cafeteria home. I wear wellington boots in the street. They are red, to make my life a bit of a celebration and so I won't get sad.

I don't enter my workplace wearing the boots. We usually leave our outside shoes at the porter's lodge. It's very convenient. I still haven't worn out a single pair of shoes I bought. I don't have to walk up and down at work. I'm a secretary. I sit at the reception and answer telephone calls. I connect the calls to whomever they ask for. I only have to connect calls to three men. I work in a small firm.

This firm belongs to Russian immigrants and they produce bottles here. What kind of bottles, I don't know. And it's not my business either, I'm a secretary, I sit in reception and usually answer calls, and whoever is wanted, I connect the telephone to them.

In general, I lead a very healthy and thrifty life.

It is true that at first I found things very difficult. Now I know

I found it difficult at the beginning because I thought I was only here temporarily. Now I know that from now on, I will always live here. That's why I'm calm these days.

At the start I had problems socialising with the woman next door because it's obvious she hates me. She hates me because I have black hair and I speak her language badly. If I was late taking my clothes off the line in the drying room, she would throw them on the floor and in the mornings I had to dry my knickers with a fan heater. For that reason, at first I was often late for work. But now I take my clothes off the line in good time and I get up an hour before work, not half an hour before. That's why I manage to get everything done, and I usually wash my knickers straight away, and that's why I always have a dry pair around.

Rainer taught me to behave like that. Rainer is a very orderly man. We usually meet on Friday evenings. To be precise, he usually comes to my place, because it's raining outside. It's also better to drink tea at home, you don't need to walk in the street in the rain, and it's cheaper too.

Rainer stays at my place on Fridays because on Saturday mornings we have sex. Sex is as necessary as bread and water. Rainer said that. I think that, for me, sex with Rainer isn't necessary at all, because whether I do or don't, it doesn't make any difference. But Rainer says that when a person doesn't have sex, he or she will become embittered. That's why on Saturday mornings, we usually have sex, as a result of which Rainer falls asleep, and, as for me, I take care of breakfast.

Once a month we go to Rainer's parents' house. Rainer's mother prepares dinner specially for us. Before our visit, Rainer always checks my outfit thoroughly. He wants me to be dressed appropriately.

Rainer's mother always cooks an excellent steak. I don't eat meat and I help myself to salad leaves.

Rainer's mother says that a woman who doesn't eat meat can't give birth to healthy children. But I can't give birth to a child anyway, because Rainer practices safe sex. But I will never tell Rainer's parents about that, because Rainer told me that they shouldn't know.

Apart from steak, Rainer's mother usually serves us hot chocolate with milk. I don't like milk, but to say no to everything would be very rude. That's why I drink hot chocolate with milk and look at photographs together with Rainer's parents. They spent one summer in Brazil and they tell me stories about that trip and show me the photographs.

It's been a long time since I was living like that.

Once Rainer's father told me that it didn't rain in Brazil and that was very good, but Rainer's mother didn't like it. Rainer's mother does not like me. She hates me. She hates me because I have black hair and I speak her language badly, and I am three months older than Rainer. She doesn't understand at all what Rainer sees in me. We have nothing in common, but I will never tell Rainer's parents that, because Rainer told me that they should not know.

It was Friday that day too, that's why Rainer was staying the night and we had sex in the morning. When Rainer turned over, I pushed my hand under the bed. I had hidden a big stone there. I took that stone and hit Rainer on the head.

After that, I threw my wellington boots out of the window and went out into the street. It was raining. I bought some cigarettes and a bottle of Russian vodka. I opened the packet and the bottle in the shop, and by the time I got home, I was very drunk.

I took my clothes off, sat in front of the mirror on the floor and carried on drinking. I was thinking about the Khde Gorge and how everything there would be as it always was, and when I go back there, soon, very soon, the elderly goat will still be there, and our old kettle, covered in soot, will be there too. Then I threw the bottle out of the window and fell asleep.

Rainer was the first to wake up. He didn't die. He reported me to the police. Nobody could get me off the charges, because Rainer had material evidence, that is his injured head and the stone with which I had hit him.

Then the doctor said that I wasn't a murderer, but insane. I was sent to the madhouse.

Nothing has changed. The walls in the room here are completely white, just like in my flat and workplace. They prepare an excellent steak here too. I don't eat meat and I help myself to salad leaves. The only difference is that that I don't have sex anymore and I am waiting for the time when I'll become embittered. I sit on the window sill and look out of the window. It's raining.

AN INSIGNIFICANT STORY OF A FAILED SUICIDE

Ira thought that God was the colour of gold. God was singing, mad with love. Ira was bending over the accordion and her thin knee almost touched her ear. She had woven cyclamen flowers into her grey hair and they were falling out, onto the accordion keyboard. 'Almighty, creator of the universe,' Ira sang, 'be kind, be gracious, show yourself to me.'

Today, Ira, a violinist from Tartu, has a lover who is twenty years of age and a make-up artist. She is adorned with tattoos up to her elbows. She's become a terrible drunkard, but when she starts singing, I usually feel like closing my eyes. Then I imagine it's a big white bird that is singing and that the bird will fly away.

***

I never discovered why she opened the door that day. Every time I asked her, she answered me with explanations that are not worth repeating. The fact is, she opened it and then immediately tried to shut it again. She didn't manage to close it, though. She was much taller than me, but I could always overpower her.

'This Georgian turned up, uninvited, this Orthodox son of a donkey. To hell with you,' she said and trudged back to her bed.

'Who's Orthodox? Me?'

Ira was never particularly concerned about her appearance, but now she was a terrible sight. Her hair was unwashed, she had a cold sore on her lip, she wore a pair of bizarre blue underpants, which she'd stuffed with something to push the fabric out where the penis should be.

I wasn't at all surprised that she was in bed. I would have

stayed in bed with great pleasure. The weather was awful, the sun never rose, and, on top of that, there was no electricity, just death and joylessness. I went to Irina's simply because I couldn't face her endless recriminations: 'You don't love me anymore,' and the like. Otherwise, what would have made me come to this distant micro-region of the city of my own free will? Let alone without even making a preliminary call. She hadn't managed to get a phone. Forget the telephone—if it hadn't been for my nagging she wouldn't even have had a lock on the toilet door. That meant either her cultured husband would have barged into the loo when I was in there, or else I would have gone in when Ira was sat there busy reading Stendhal.

This time, neither Stendhal nor Ira's concoction for gargling, made with seven herbs, was to be seen anywhere. Ira drank this seven-herb stuff in incredible doses and she foisted it on to her husband and daughter, saying, 'It's delicious!' Yes, very, what can you say? Ugh.

This time, as I mentioned, she wasn't reading anything, wasn't drinking anything, and neither did she speak to me. She had turned over to face the wall.

I went to take my fur jacket off, but then I changed my mind. It was cold.

'Ira?'

She was crying. Why was I surprised? I had seen Ira crying before, but at those times she had cried differently, shedding tears like a silly cartoon princess. This time, though, she was crying quietly, so miserably that I felt my heart breaking.

'Hey.'

Suddenly I thought that her husband had beaten her up. I don't know why that thought popped into my head. If I prayed to God all my life long, I would never get a husband like Ira's, he was a special man. As my friend's father once said, how is it that Ira's convict father should have such a son-in-law and I'm left with sod-all? But lately we've all gone a little mad from cold and poverty, and perhaps her husband has lost his marbles too?

I squatted near her bed and became convinced that there was definitely something gravely wrong. She gave off a sour odour, the kind you get in the rooms of elderly patients. She was pushing her tangled head of hair into the pillow and hiding her face, silly Irochka. She was saying something that I could barely decipher.

'Come on, speak up, Ira! Are you possessed by the devil?'

'If I am, what can I do?'

I laughed.

Poor old Irochka, whatever she said made me laugh. She became infuriated by my laughter and that made me laugh even more. It seems I'm a moron too.

Apparently, three days ago, Ira decided that she was full of ennui and she didn't want to live. She couldn't explain exactly what she was bored of and it seems she was bored of everything. That's why she decided to commit suicide. She had always been a very clever woman.

She rejected the idea of jumping out of the window immediately as she felt sorry for her child. It's true that it wouldn't be nice to see Mom's corpse like that. Next she ruled out the idea of hanging herself. She couldn't possibly climb a tree to do it. In fact, she couldn't climb a tree at all because the truth is she could barely climb the stairs. Never mind hanging herself, she'd never even managed to hang a picture. Some of them were on the top of the wardrobe, and some of them leaned against the wall. Everything was topsy-turvy in her house. It takes courage to cut one's wrists and Ira was terribly afraid of pain. I didn't need to be told—before the dentist could do anything in her mouth she would crush my hands from fear. She'd crush them so hard she'd break bones. Pills? Yes, she'd had already a bad experience with tablets, but I didn't know that. Apparently the most she achieved was that she threw up, and after that had a headache but she still hadn't managed to kill herself.

So, Irochka decided that she should starve herself to death and I was the poor soul who witnessed the third day of this heroic endeavour.

At first, I thought she was playing the fool as usual, blurting out silly things. But she didn't stop and I realized that the situation really was critical. On top of that, I wasn't able to console her at all, because she wasn't saying anything that could be denied. Actually, she never lied at all. Think about it. She said, 'My husband doesn't love me anymore.' And that was logical, because if he did, he would realise that this woman, whether cleverly or stupidly (makes no difference), was committing suicide. And the child too, it was the third day that her daughter had been sent to Granny Yelena. The daughter obviously preferred to be with the people of that class where no one tells her off if she chooses to eat straight from the saucepan. She could cope without her mother, and in fact, she might find it relaxing. Besides, she was already grown up and what had Ira got to look forward to? The time when her daughter becomes a whore or the time when she gets married? What if she does neither? Well then, would she join a convent or what? That would be even better!

And Ira was angry that until today, I hadn't given her any proper advice. I wonder what I should have said. Should I have suggested she get a lover, or what? That would be stupid, my dear. Your husband is way better than anyone else. He's always around and doesn't get on anyone's nerves. As for the rest, well, whatever, everyone does that in the same way.

What else? I've got an idea! Perhaps you should go travelling again? I'll come with you. Well, what else do I have to do? I don't know, we'll go somewhere. What, didn't you enjoy it when you travelled before? Do you remember how much we danced at Bitkha, when Avramiko was beating the drum? There were glowworms there. Anyway, Avramiko was very keen on you. What did you want from him? He was such a beautiful boy. Okay, we won't be able to travel in the Soviet Union, and we don't have enough money to go anywhere else, but if you want, we can definitely go somewhere.

'Yes, let's go to Grozny. Or to Gagra in Abkhazia. Perhaps they'll recognize you as Georgian because of your Georgian face, and they'll hang us somewhere.'

'Okay, go without me.'

'What nonsense are you saying?'

'Dunno. But what can I do?'

It got dark. Why don't they light candles in this house? I bumped into everything. Ira, of course, couldn't care less. On the contrary, I think, she was delighted.

'I couldn't give a shit. I wish you'd broken your foot.'

'Ira, I'll go, but you know, if you die now, you'll go to hell.'

How could I have said that? She suddenly lifted her head. I was frightened. What had happened?

'If I live a long and happy life does that mean I'll be sent straight to heaven?' she asked in Russian.

***

The mailboxes that were out of use had their doors open and they were banging and creaking in the wind. Who needs mailboxes anyway? A dog started yapping. If the dog attacks me and bites me, how I'd laugh. That dog's an idiot.

THERE, IN THE NORTH

My fat friend used to begin every morning by having a moan.

'Why am I here?'

'Well, dear, how would I know?'

'I know! Because crazy people live here! Like him, he's crazy, he killed his own mother!'

'No, he didn't. It was the other one who killed his mother, the one with glasses!'

'Big deal! But he did kill someone.'

Yes, he really did kill someone. He'd been both in prison and in the madhouse. Now, he was here. Fatty wasn't lying at all. And indeed, why were we, two adult, healthy Georgian women, here in the madhouse?

'I can't begin to understand them! Where did this rotten one take my rotten slippers?'

I was the rotten one. I was wearing slippers. But, in fact, they were my own slippers.

We probably weren't totally healthy either, otherwise, why would we have ended up here? Or how could we bear to be here? And, yet, somehow we managed to bear it. With varying degrees of success, but nevertheless we bore it.

When I had some free time, I usually hurried to Romas's place. Fatty called Romas 'the dirty one.' And he really was dirty. But he hadn't really killed his mother. His mother lived in the capital, I knew her, she was an opera singer. She was even fatter than my Fatty.

Romas, who had been thrown out of the family home, had a good, two-story house in our hamlet. It was the smallest, that's why it was easy to get it warm. In the evenings we roasted potatoes in a *burzhuika*, an old metal stove, and listened to Pink Floyd. The record was scratched. Romas had a Rigonda record player that was about a hundred years old. A green light came on and you had to wait until the green light was really bright which meant the old thing was properly warmed up and ready to use.

That autumn we painted all the chairs at Romas's house in different colours. Everywhere stank of acetone. I painted masses of swastikas then, one day, when we'd run out of chairs and we were sanding down the table, a gawky woman opened the door. She started shouting something in her language and Romas told me it would be better for me if I left. After that he only phoned me once. He was already in the capital and told me that he and his wife were going to Finland. Poor old Romas.

Fatty used to go running in the forest. I think her speed was around fifty centimeters an hour. In the evening, she drank milk. 'It helps me think,' she said. We could see the huge pine trees from our windows and also a sculpture depicting a mother and child, a remnant from the Soviet era. From time to time, young boys appeared in the bushes outside, and Fatty would close the curtains. 'I won't give you the pleasure,' she used to say.

On the other hand, why not let them enjoy themselves, if they found such things enjoyable? Surely it's enough that we didn't enjoy anything. The only thing I enjoyed was eating, because the cook, Vika, prepared delicious meals, as long as she wasn't on a diet.

That cook Vika was the most spoiled, badly behaved and useless woman I had ever met. Neither her body nor her face were remarkable, and certainly not her behaviour. She came from Norilsk and was really foul-mouthed. But, as I said, her food could be nice. There had to be at least one thing she could do well.

Actually, I'm lying. She also did something else well, and that was Janine. Janine was her daughter and she resembled an angel, or a fairy, I don't know what. She was a miracle—blonde, with dark brown eyes; everything about her was beautiful. I could never understand how that idiot Vika gave birth to a girl like her. For the first time, I realised that God's munificence wasn't evenly distributed. Also, you should have seen Janine's father. He visited his ex-wife and his daughter twice. His appearance and temperament resembled peeled potatoes, and Fatty, after she'd met him, said that he must have been brought up on fat-free porridge. Fatty herself couldn't stand fair-skinned men and she was impressed by the darkest, hairiest, and the most hopelessly macho guys. She even liked my dirty Romas more than Janine's father. 'Romas is okay,' she said. 'At least he's got a good laugh on him.'

No one knows why someone decided to give this poor child an exotic name like Janine when she lived in prosaic Norilsk. When I asked Vika, she told me that she used to listen to the French songs of Mireille Mathieu back then and that was why. That's crazy logic. I think it was because I nagged her that Vika liked me, or rather she tried to befriend me. It gave her some kind of masochistic pleasure. She thought that, if I could be bothered to argue with her, I must love her too. It wasn't that at all. Vika made me want to throw up, just like all the other inhabitants of that house made me sick. Except, of course, Fatty.

In spite of the fact that Vika tried to make me a 'best friend,' and used to tell me incredible stories whenever she caught up with me, I had nothing to do with her daughter. I never spoke to her. Probably because I'm not mad about children and I don't know how I should treat them. I'm either afraid, or I don't know what to do. Also, my nervous system was in a bad way, so I had little patience with whining brats, and Janine was four years old.

When it snowed so much that Fatty couldn't go running and Romas was taken to Finland by his bogeyman of a wife, we finally flipped and became the star attraction at our asylum. We sang the song about the wounded crane's sorry adventures at the top of our voices. We went round muddling up the shoes that had been left outside our neighbours' doors, and so on. Then Fatty said that we had to avoid going completely mad, as it was shameful, and eventually she bought a supply of valerian.

It was thanks to this valerian that I first spoke to Janine. We'd been drinking this blessed brew with no results whatsoever out of a three-liter jar. A lot of leaves remained so I decided to throw a party for the local cats to brighten up a gloomy winter's evening. I put on the trainers I was so proud of, the ones Fatty disrespectfully referred to as 'orthopaedic,' and climbed over our balcony with the jar in my hand. I headed for the sculpture celebrating motherhood, which was precisely illuminated by the light from our window. When I finally reached it, I threw the remaining valerian all over the mother's torso and breasts. And then I headed back.

That's when I saw Janine. She was standing at the foot of our staircase, in the snow. She wasn't wearing her jacket.

'What are you doing?' she asked me in English. I knew that she spoke English and Estonian. Russian was unintelligible to her, although her mother only spoke Russian, and bad Russian at that. I'd never heard anything like it, but that's how it was.

'What are you doing? Aren't you cold?'

'No.'

I climbed on to the balcony and took Janine with me. She weighed as little as a bird. When I put my arms around her, I was frightened that I might break something in her body. Fatty opened the door.

'Who's that?'

'I'm Janine. What made you do that?'

Well, with my brilliant English, how could I possibly explain? It was Fatty who helped me. She explained everything to Janine about the relationship between cats and valerian and how our nervous system works. She also made a comparative analysis of Georgian and Northern climates. Janine watched her with her mouth open, and I realised from the movement of her lips that she was repeating the words to herself. I don't know how much she understood.

We switched off the light and nestled on the window sill. After a while the first pussycat arrived.

'Here she comes,' whispered Janine.

The cat had real problems. The snow was deep and obviously it couldn't step into my footprints. As it took some steps forward, it would shake itself in disgust. But eventually it seemed it gave up resisting and very quickly and efficiently reached the fragrant breasts of the sculpture celebrating motherhood, which were strewn with valerian. Then the second cat appeared, then the third and so on.

If my guardian angel hadn't been either frozen or asleep, just like the inhabitants of that area, he would certainly have been pleased with me, and those cats would have been full of gratitude too. All the cats of the entire neighbourhood were now rolling around on the sculpture. Then they started fighting and, after that, began yowling.

'It's amazing!' Janine didn't move an inch. She was still squatting on the window sill. She really did look like a bird.

'What's amazing?'

She looked up at me. 'I know better English than you do.'

Everyone knows better English than me.

She crawled down off the window sill and moved towards the door. Not to the garden door but the door into the corridor. Fatty accompanied her and quietly told her something that sounded like a very long sentence. I couldn't make out what was said.

'Don't worry,' Janine answered, and left.

Fatty cursed all night long. When she woke up, she continued swearing and went off to wash, cursing and swearing all the way.

'What can you expect from a whore from Norilsk? Norilsk is such a flat wasteland.'

'Is it really?'

'Of course it is. Did you think it was the Himalayas? She must have grown up in a burrow like a desert rat.'

The topic of Vika's upbringing, education and moral standing was soon forgotten because the mad people prepared fresh joys for us every day. We usually had fun with their adventures. Sometimes, though, we were personally involved, and that could be unpleasant.

We had a cleaner called Vitiok, with bright red hair and so many gold teeth that Fatty called him the Gold Mine. He was a typical throwback to the Soviet hippy era. He was slightly madder than was desirable and claimed to have some knowledge of Buddhism, as well as rather bold sexual demands. He was hale and hearty, and mopped the floors in a vigorous manner, singing in a style that was both loud and self-sacrificing. *Ah my lovely voice, ah my lovely hair, Vitka's washing the corridors.* One morning we found a note stuck on Vitiok's door, saying in English, 'Goodbye forever,' and, underneath, a massive number of obscene words and pictures. I wasn't worried that Vitiok had left; he'd left and that was that, but it was decided that before they could appoint a new cleaner, we would have to take turns to mop the floors.

I hate work like that. I'd rather be asked to chop down all the trees in the whole park. But Fatty explained to me that dirty jobs purified the human soul, and that physical labour was better than sitting around reading tea leaves. So, my life developed more variety. For nearly a whole year, twice a week, in the afternoon, I first had to sweep and, after that, to mop nearly three hundred square meters of floor. I suddenly understood Vitiok very well, and I started singing too, with the same ardour, and in deference to him, I went for the classical repertoire. *I married her and now I'll take her doggy style.*

Fatty had a different repertoire. *The wind is moving the reeds in the familiar riverbed.* She went along polishing the floor softly with a cloth. She called her vocal style 'lyric soprano.'

'Is that a Georgian song?' the mother-murderer asked me.

'No,' I answered, 'It's classical jazz.'

'Ah.'

'Aha.' I was still afraid of this bloke and used to smile appeasingly at him, in case he didn't like me for some reason and killed me too.

This floor washing, as I've already told you, was interminable. I remember Janine coming up to me; it was the end of autumn, so the floor was especially muddy. I was squeezing out the cloth and feeling hatred towards everybody.

'What are you doing?'

I opened out the cloth and wrapped it around the mop.

'You know what?'

'What?' When I straightened up, I laughed. She really was minute and was looking at me very seriously with slightly parted lips. A man I met not so long ago has the same way of looking at me. He probably thinks I'm a fool because I laugh all the time. He really does remind me of Janine. The only difference is that he is big, and also a man.

'Here, stand on top of the mop. No, squat down on it and I'll push you along. Would you like that?' Berta Solomonovna used to give me a ride like that, when I was Janine's age. I thought she did it to give me a nice time, but a neighbour, a nasty woman, explained that having something heavy on the mop helped to clean the floor more effectively.

'Yes. I would.'

For some reason, she stretched out her hand and I took it. Janine stepped onto the mop with the grace of a real queen. Then she squatted down.

'Hold on to the handle.'

'Yes.'

We started moving along and Janine began to giggle. I saw

her laughing for the first time. She was squeezing her shoulders together as if someone invisible was tickling her. It was impossible to see her eyes at all as they shrunk with laughter. Berta Solomonovna must have been an expert in this business. I went straight away to the end of the corridor.

'More?'

'No more.'

'That's fine, no problem.' And off she went.

I told Fatty this story over supper. Janine was sitting in the distance with her mouth open, listening to a conversation between her mother and Mortena, one of the warders. I don't know what they were talking about as I don't understand Estonian. I could tell, though, that it wasn't good.

'She's a lovely kid,' said Fatty. Then she started swearing about Janine's mother again, using such foul language I won't write it down.

On the following day, Fatty had to travel to Moscow to take some exams. She got up at the crack of dawn and went to the bus station.

I swear before God that her departure upset me a bit. I don't always like to be completely on my own. And, besides, Fatty was a good companion and she never got on my nerves. I wish I could meet a man like that.

That's what I was thinking about when someone opened the door without knocking. It seems that there isn't a custom of knocking before entering in Norilsk. And in barged Vika. I was so surprised that I didn't even remonstrate. She came in, sat on the bed and told me such a miraculous thing that I was struck dumb.

Vika told me that Janine said she'd had a good time with me yesterday. And she, Vika, had decided to go to Moscow together with Fatty because she had some business there, but her business was such that she couldn't take Janine with her. So she would leave Janine with me and would be back in two weeks. Now she had to run or she'd miss the bus. Bye!

In my entire long life I can remember only two occasions when I really was rendered speechless. Once in a lift in a hostel in Donetsk—a lanky black man offered me sex for five dollars, meaning I had to pay the five dollars. The second time this Victoria managed to do it.

So she left Janine with me. I was in a complete panic.

I thought I would get up, have a wash, recover my senses and afterwards have a think about what the hell I could do. But I didn't get a chance to catch my breath, let alone relax. Janine was waiting for me in the communal bathroom. She was trying to take her sweater off and her head had gotten stuck.

'Hey, Janine!'

She managed to pull the sweater off over her head in a flash and stared at me.

'What do you want?'

I told her that her that her mother had decided to go to Moscow together with Fatty, because she had some business there, but the business was such that she could not take Janine with her. She had left Janine with me and would return in two weeks' time, and that she'd had to run or the bus would leave without her. I felt terribly sorry for Janine and also for my beloved self.

'Okay,' she said so obediently, I was absolutely touched. While I got undressed I stole a glance at her. She put her clean clothes neatly on the chair, she took her tiny toothbrush from her bag, she moved an upside-down clothes box across to the sink. At first I was concerned that the box might break, but there was no need, because Janine barely weighed anything. I reached for the sweater which had been thrown on the floor. Janine looked at me and said, 'Leave it, I'll take care of it.'

On our first evening together, Janine announced, 'Good night' and headed towards her room to sleep.

'Aren't you going to stay with me?'

'What for?'

'Because I don't like to sleep alone.'

She looked at me suspiciously. But in fact I wasn't really lying, so probably that's why she believed me. 'I'm afraid. You know that my friend stayed with me before, but now she's in Moscow. Stay. Please, Janine!'

She became pensive. 'What are you afraid of?'

'I don't know.' It wasn't a particularly instructive answer, but it was all I could think of.

'I know, you can sleep at my place. It would be better like that.'

Janine never caused any problems. She washed herself, dressed herself, tied up her hair—in a rather strange way, but so tidily, you couldn't criticise her. She also washed her underwear while she took a bath so that dirty underwear didn't accumulate. She told me to tell her when I was putting my washing into the washing machine so she could put hers in too.

She didn't have any toys and she didn't want any. She didn't know any fairy tales either. I still don't know how you say 'fairy tale' in English and that's why I told her that I would tell her a story.

'What for?'

'I don't know. For fun.'

My 'Little Red Riding Hood' became 'Little Red Dress,' but that's neither here nor there. I remembered how I was afraid of the wolf, and how I was sorry for him when he was disembowelled. I always demanded they tell me 'Little Red Riding Hood' without the wolf. That's why I told Janine that they sewed the wolf's tummy back up, and afterwards he gave his word that he would never touch little girls and old grannies again.

I was lying on the floor, Janine was listening to me, bending down from the bed. When I finished she did not utter a word, but she was still watching me. Then she crawled across to me and sat at my feet.

'Do you believe that?' she asked.

'Believe what?'

'That he won't eat them anymore.'

'I don't know, he gave his word, didn't he?'

'So what? He's still a wolf.'

'I don't know, Janine, I haven't heard of him eating anyone else.'

'Really?'

'Yes.'

During the day, she hung around me all the time, but didn't touch me. She was usually talking to herself and making her own entertainment. It gave me some pangs of conscience. When I was her age, I had a hundred people doting over me. I had thousands of friends, but I still grew up useless. I didn't know what I could do. Then I found three ribbons amongst Fatty's supplies. I wondered what on earth she needed them for. I wove them around the top of a chair. I remember when I was in Pasanauri my mum taught me how to make plaits. Janine mastered the technique immediately and while I spent sleepless nights watching the blue-screened Olivet, she, with her tiny fingers, plaited over and over again. She would undo them and then start again, then she asked me if she could do my hair like that. I said she could. Even if she left out bits, creating tufts, I would not say a word. She sat on the back of the chair and, while I occupied myself with something, she plaited my hair. She made a perfect job of it.

In the evenings, when I'd finished the housework and washing the floors, we would go out for a walk. She wouldn't hold my hand or anything. The only thing was that I had to move slowly because Janine was very small.

'If you like we could run through the leaves?'

'What for?' She looked at me with her mouth open.

'They make a rustling sound and it's fun.'

'We'll get dirty.'

'So what?'

She ran after me and giggled. She tried to throw the leaves at me, but her little fists couldn't hold very many. She fell into a pile of leaves, she laughed and rolled around.

'Come on! It's such fun!'

On the way back I asked her whether she was tired and if she wanted me to carry her. She answered not to worry as there wasn't much further to walk.

Well, really there wasn't much time left. It was running out. But anyway, I loved Janine as much as it was possible for me to love anyone. And she never changed at all from the day I first met her. She didn't entirely trust me, but looked at me all the time with interest, with her mouth slightly open, looking incredibly beautiful.

In the evenings they played the organ in the cathedral. 'Hey, Janine, would you like to go?'

'Is it good?'

'I don't know, I like it. And we can light some candles too.'

'What for?'

'I don't know. They look beautiful.'

'Okay, let's see.'

We decided we should dress up. Janine minced along to her room, saying she would get dressed and wait for me outside. I looked at my miserable wardrobe. I no longer knew what dressing up meant. Whom should I dress up for? For Fatty? And yet it would be awkward to go to the cathedral wearing Romas's old jeans.

In the end, of course, I still put on the jeans and went out into the garden. Janine was still not to be seen.

It was already dark, but it wasn't yet as cold as it usually gets there. It was a nice evening.

What a horror that motherhood sculpture is. Seeing it, you wouldn't want either your mother or anything else. Then I realized that Janine was taking ages. What could she be putting on that would take so long? I returned to the house. The door was locked. I couldn't believe it. I knocked. 'Janine?'

Then I rushed into the garden again.

'Janine, Janine!'

'Here I am.' She was sitting in a bush and was crying, wiping her tears with her fists. I nearly went crazy.

'What's wrong? Who's upset you? Janine!' I took her in my arms. She was like a little pebble, tense and very frightened.

To cut a long story short, apparently she'd wanted to pee and she'd wet the dress she'd decorated herself. 'Never mind, come on, we'll change it.' I only realised later that she thought I would beat her.

Would I beat Janine? I'd kill anyone who upset Janine. I said to her, 'What do you think, that I wouldn't be able to fight? What nonsense! Would you like me to uproot this tree? No? Then if you like, I'll beat up Mortena, the warder, the one who is standing over there. No? So who do you want me to beat up?'

She started laughing. 'Why are you laughing? Hey, Janine, we'll be late for the concert!'

And we were late too. But we didn't want to go back either. We spent some time walking around the lake. I taught her a Georgian nonsense rhyme—*Neli, neli, pioneri*—but what a stupid thing to do. Finally we sat on the long bench. It was wet, but I took the hood off my fur jacket, sat on that and took Janine in my lap.

The street lights were reflected in the lake. There was only one swan swimming around. In summer there were lots of them. It was a big, white swan, swimming near the bank.

'It would be good if we had some bread now, we could have given it to the swan.'

'Yes,' said Janine, 'But it's very big, isn't it?'

'Yes, it is big.'

The swan came up to the bank. To tell the truth, I didn't like the look of it.

It really was very big and it had the ugliest legs. For some reason it headed in our direction.

Janine leaned into me with her back. She became tense.

'Don't be frightened. Can't you see how thin its neck is? It isn't strong.'

And suddenly that horrible bird flapped its wings. It really was enormous. Janine broke loose from me and ran into the forest. She trusted her legs more than me. How horrible, my God!

She stood with her fists clenched. I squatted in front of her.

'Now tell me what you've done.'

Janine looked at me guiltily. Then she slowly came closer to me. She tried to hug me and said quietly:

'I'm sorry I left you, were you very frightened?'

When we returned home, the door of my room was open. Fatty and Vika were waiting for me, sitting on my bed. They'd returned.

Fatty, of course had successfully passed her exams. What Vika did, I don't know. Fatty said, 'Fuck her,' and she said some other stuff too, only it was very bad so I won't write it down.

Janine didn't speak to me. She didn't even look at me. It was only three days later she came to my room and stood at the door. She and her mother were going to Moscow. She wore a new fur jacket.

'What's up, Janine?'

'Nothing, you carry on working.'

'Are you wearing a new fur jacket?'

'Yes.'

I felt like an idiot. And I was an idiot.

'You know what?' she asked me when she was leaving.

'What?'

'My English is better than yours.'

Everyone knows English better than I do.

MARINA'S BIRTHDAY

As well as her many other remarkable attributes, Madame Nora (yes, Madame Nora, not Granny Nora) had one particular virtue. She would start to talk either when Marina was in an especially good mood, or else when she was very tired. In other words, at those times when it was least necessary.

Madame Nora, who was about a thousand years old, claimed that in her youth she was 'beautiful beyond God,' and when she came out on to the street, to her left, men would fall down from sheer love, and to her right, women's hearts would burst from jealousy. Obviously, all sixteen-year-olds are attractive, so probably Nora too looked pretty good as she was tall and long-legged. But as for 'beautiful beyond God,' there was no evidence for that, not even in photographs, and certainly nothing now remained except her endless self-regard.

Madame preferred her own self over and above everyone else. During her long life no one could convince her that there was anyone in the world who was her equal. For the last ten years, no one had attempted to prove otherwise to her and it had become absolutely impossible to socialise with her. That's why Marina had to put up with everything, including Nora's godless beauty, her opinions, her insistence on ecologically pure food, her menthol cigarettes, and even her white collars.

Marina was plain, and different from Nora, and no one knew that better than she did. You probably know a lot of women like her. There was nothing particularly wrong with her looks that many others didn't also share, yet she was ugly. She was short, but you wouldn't say she was petite and neat. She was slim, but she had thick bones and a primitive build. She had dark, yellowish skin and neither a suntan nor make-up suited her. Her hair always looked unwashed. I don't know what else to mention. To put it bluntly, she was ugly.

When you are ugly and an orphan, and, in addition, they failed to pay your wages, and your man fell in love with another woman, you have nothing to be happy about. And if you add the fact that you live in Tbilisi, and your mother is half-Russian and half-Armenian, with both nationalities having a sense of superiority, then life could hardly get better! But if you add in a Madame Nora at home who cares about money and a man, then, really, everything's over.

But the existence of Nora did have one positive side. It was always warm in the house and she would not have instant coffee or tea bags, but the real thing. A similar principle applied to the whole kitchen. Besides, Nora slept a lot, like a top model, as Marina's ex would say, and that's why in the morning nobody bugged Marina's brain in the kitchen. She could sit quietly and drink her first cup of coffee in bliss.

But that day she did not stand a chance of enjoying such pleasure. The coffee wasn't yet brewed when the telephone rang. Marina picked up the receiver. The Soviet Minsk refrigerator rattled, the coffee got spilled, Marina staggered to her feet, knocking the chair over, and Nora woke up.

'Who was that?' she called. Marina was worried.

'Calm down,' Marina muttered to herself.

'Who was that?'

'Wrong number.'

'Who was calling, what did they say?'

'What do you want, Nora?'

Nora was now standing in the doorway. She was wrapped in a pink fluffy dressing gown, was wearing embroidered slippers, and her black hair was all tangled.

'What a nightmare,' thought Marina.

'Did you ask why they were calling?'

'No.'

'Why not?'

'Why should I have done?'

'Why are you talking to me in this manner?'

'What do you want, Nora?'

'When will they give you the money?'

Marina sat down. The nagging had started.

'Shall I make you coffee?'

'No! When will they give you the money?'

'At the end of the month. In a week. Do you want anything?'

'What should I want? I simply want to know when they will give you the money.'

At one stage, there were several topics of conversation that Marina vetoed, including discussion of her looks and Beso. Nora knew that touching on one or another of these themes would end up with swearing and dishes being smashed, but because no one had sworn at her yet about the subject of money, she carried on and on.

'Noriko, come on!'

'What do you mean "come on"?'

'Nora!'

'Shall I make coffee for you?'

That was Noriko's way. First she would drive you crazy and then, very pleased with herself, would leave you alone.

***

Marina hated celebrations such as New Year, Easter and her own birthday. She hated them basically because, for many years, she had waited like an idiot for someone to greet her with a gift or something. No, some people did congratulate her, but the one person she wanted to be congratulated by, didn't. Beso, specifically.

In general, Beso was very attentive and a nice guy, it was simply that he celebrated New Year with his friends, and at Easter he went to the monastery. You wouldn't believe the bad luck, but Marina's birthday was on the same day as Beso's sister's. The day after, Beso would have a hangover, and on the third day he would take Marina out somewhere. Well, as I said, he was a very nice guy. But Marina wasn't happy on the third day either. She was rather an ungrateful woman, our Marina.

At that moment, though, the problem was irrelevant, because Beso wouldn't take her anywhere. Beso had fallen in love with another woman. Nevertheless, Marina still hated her birthday. And today was her birthday. Not only that, it was Sunday.

***

At the time when she was still friends with Beso, Marina had a lot to do. She made the epilating machine roar loudly in order to irritate Noriko. And in an attempt to make this same Nora's heart burst, she would spend money recklessly. She attended a slimming club which required that she didn't eat before going to bed, which meant she didn't bother to cook supper for her beloved old lady either. For these and for many other reasons, Nora could not stand Beso.

No, it never occurred to her that Beso might marry Marina and that, if he did, he would deprive Nora of something. She didn't worry about that at all, because she was firmly convinced that nobody would take Marina from her, given that she had such poor looks and low breeding. Nora couldn't stand it when Beso called her Granny Nora, obviously being deliberately over-familiar. Nor could she bear the way Beso yelled for Marina from the yard, on the pretext that Nora didn't want to see him, but probably knowing full well that Nora was asleep. So what if it was daytime? Besides, Marina was usually with Beso twice a week at least, and, in spite of Nora's moaning that she had a headache, backache, and an ingrowing toenail, she would still go, that ungrateful wench of an Armenian mother. Then, that pervert Beso sent a book to Noriko called *Anti-Carnegie or Man Manipulator*, and Nora finally flipped. Then Beso disappeared.

'Where did he go?' asked Nora.

'I don't know.'

'I told you he would go, didn't I? What did you expect? I'm surprised that he hung around with you for so many years! Shame, he was such a handsome guy!' said Nora.

'Nora, have I done something to upset you?'

'That's got nothing to do with it,' replied Nora. 'It's about time you understood something. You're forty years old! Okay, thirty-five.'

And from today, thirty-six, Madame Eleonora. You simply don't remember that any more.

On the other hand, Nora knew very well that she shouldn't have mentioned Beso again that day. She wouldn't admit it, but when Marina made a scene, it had a big effect on her. In truth, she was secretly delighted when Marina shouted, or banged the walls and the table, or when she yelled at some neighbour who came to the door. So when Noriko was having a heart attack about it all, she was giving it to herself. Whichever it was, by then Marina couldn't give a shit. Bravo Marina! She'd learned something from Nora. But she should have reprimanded Beso. And why did she shout at Nora? But, still ...

***

How nice that it's getting dark early! thought Marina. How nice that Nora loved watching soap operas! How nice that those who were supposed to phone actually phoned when she wasn't expecting anyone!

Nora is a so-and-so! She didn't once ask why I kept saying

'thank you' all the time to people who phoned. She couldn't care less. Thank God.

The Minsk fridge went silent. The sound of a television came from the living room. Marina was laying on her small sofa and looked at the ceiling. It was warm. How nice! She remembered a dream. She had had it a while back, at the time she was friends with Beso. In the dream, she was lying the same way, only she knew that she was in the earth. Her mother and father were buried at her head. When she told Beso about it, he laughed and said that her father would live for another thousand years, what could kill him? So the dream meant that he would not die yet. Anyway, her mother and father lay there, and here lay Marina. It wasn't a cemetery, she could see some kind of rampart and a field, as if she were looking down from above. It was misty, probably the end of November, but it was warm. A colt ran around the field, and for some reason it had a beard. She had seen a colt like that in a village called Pasanauri in the mountains when she went there with Beso.

Then she was told that when it grew, it would lose its beard and would become an ordinary horse. So, there was a colt running around, it was foggy, Marina was lying and thinking, How nice! It will probably snow soon and then it will get even warmer.

'Are you asleep?'

'What is it?'

'Nothing. I just want to know whether you're asleep or not.'

'Not any more.'

The telephone rang. 'Minsk' started rattling.

'Who was that?'

'They hung up.'

'Why are they phoning? What did they say?'

'What do you want, Nora?'

RIKHALSKI'S HOUSE

On 7th March 1913, Ekaterine Rikhalskaya, daughter of Fyodor, submitted a statement to Tbilisi City Council. She was applying for planning permission to build a two-story house with a cellar on the land which belonged to her. To the north, the house would be next to Gunibi Street, to the east, Matinovski Street, and to the south and west it would abut Madame Matinovski's land. An engineer called Kharadze was responsible for the construction.

I've always known that I owned a flat in a building on Barnov Street. I was taken there by my parents as a child, and then the building seemed to me like some kind of huge chasm. Hanging on the wall was a stuffed squirrel, showing its teeth, and at the entrance a tap was rattling. In the building where I grew up, the walls were immense and the ceilings were nearly five meters high. Half of the walls were taken up by the windows, and that's probably why, as a child, I thought I'd never live in that Barnov house. It wasn't a house designed for human beings to live in. That's what I thought, but I was very much mistaken.

Several years ago, when I ran out of money, I became interested in that Barnov place. I thought I would sell it. When I found out its true story, I didn't sell it and I never will. Yes, I'm sentimental, but so what?

At first, I was frightened of going there. That's why I asked the painter, Guga Kotetishvili to accompany me. I'll be forever grateful to him. Guga shoved his hand into a horrible-looking hole (he was generally a very brave chap) and informed me that that building had an air channel or pipe, I don't know what to call it, running along the entire external wall, and that's why it would never suffer from damp. Later we extracted a lot of rubbish from

99

that pipe way, and we also discovered ventilation channels in the flat. There was a small metal ornamental door from which a brick had fallen out, which meant I couldn't get the door to budge at all.

Even now I'm still embarrassed in front of Guga, when I remember how, when I opened the shutters and some feathers fell down, I panicked and probably behaved terribly, like a really silly woman. Now I know that they were turtledove feathers, a nice bird, which it appears has a nest in the cypress tree. The cypress tree is right in front of the window and so it makes sense that feathers would fall down there, doesn't it? But at the time, I was really frightened and all kinds of ideas came into my mind, such as black magic and thousands of other bad omens. Besides, as well as the flat being dark and in a diabolical state, the previous night I had had a dream. In the dream, a woman opened the door, and when I asked her who the hell she was, she answered that she was Ivanova and that she lived there. I know that Ivanova had been a tenant and that she had died here. And so, why was she appearing now? But Guga could not care less about such things, and he carefully explained to me that my basement flat had great potential, if it were renovated.

Ever since I stepped into this place, superstitions, legends and rituals have been following me all the time. It wasn't just Madame Ivanova, but I knew for certain, even if I don't know how, that one of the previous owners, Mr Rakovich, had died in my very room. I remembered a proverb, too, that says a church without a master will be taken over by devils. That's why, before I began the renovations, I lit a fire in every room. You know that fire cleanses everything. At least that's my opinion. Besides, it's fun to watch and imagine monsters and evil spirits running away screaming and yelling. Someone suggested bringing in a priest, but I didn't want someone splashing holy water around my lovely place, and I'm not mad about bearded men either.

And this is the legend. The building which is now called No. 64 Barnov Street, together with the brick-built house in front of it, was built by a Polish colonel called Rikhalski. He built it for his daughters, who had consumption, a fact which, for some reason, every narrator stresses. In the documents dating from 1945, the Colonel is named as Rikhalevski, but elsewhere the building is in the name of Ekaterine Rikhalski. To cut a long story short, there's a big confusion. Probably, it would be better to trust Madame Ekaterine's handwritten document. She perhaps knew better than anyone else that she was a Rikhalskaya and nothing else.

I can't tell you whether Ekaterine had consumption or not, or where her illness had come from. I have my doubts, and by expressing them I am contributing to the oral folklore of the Vera district of Tbilisi. At that time, members of the lice-ridden general population were beside themselves with envy that a Polish woman should be so rich and beautiful. The cypress tree garden is usually cited as a proof of the woman's illness. I don't even know how Mr Rakovich came to marry the daughter of Rikhalski and what passions were circulating in the air. The fact is that Rakovich was already the owner of another house in Barnov Street—48a. Not only did he get the very lovely Ekaterine and the house, he was lucky enough to get the most famous cypress and lilac garden in Tbilisi.

Thanks to my neighbours, the lilac is still blooming and the garden exists too, smaller than at the beginning of the last century, but nevertheless lovely. Of the remaining cypress trees, one, as I mentioned before, is growing above my window and the turtle dove still lives in it. This turtle dove has bred and her descendants leave their droppings on my kitchen doorstep. There's nothing I can do. I can't throw stones at them, can I? That drives me insane. I would love to throw stones at these native birds of Vera, but if I hit one, it will die, and if I miss it, I'll break the neighbour's window. Both outcomes would be shameful and a disgrace.

Rakovich and Rikhalskaya had a daughter called Elene. As well as legends about this lady, we also have some facts. To this day, people in Vera remember that she was a remarkably beautiful woman, an artist, and that her husband, Mr Dzigurov, was sent to Turkey as a diplomat. The Rikhalski house technically belonged to him and the people who were settled there had the status of tenants. Elene never said anything derogatory about these people. According to her they were cultured, and not members of the dirty proletariat, like some of the people settled in other houses during Soviet times.

There's only one book where this house, more precisely a house with this name, is mentioned. This book is called *The Country of Lemonade* by Jaba Ioseliani. I asked Mr Jaba to tell me something about the house. Mr Jaba had the same story to tell as I did. At one stage he used to live in the building too, on the floor above mine. Then it became clear that the chest of drawers that Mr Jaba's mother sold while moving out of the apartment had previously been bought by someone called Marlenov (his name being an abbreviation of Marx-Lenin). Before the revolution, it had belonged to a man called Nakhichkarian, from the highest Guild of Merchants. After that, it appears Marlenov also experienced hardship, and the chest of drawers, with its characteristic scratches and dents, ended up on Barnov Street again—in my flat. Currently, it's the most ancient inhabitant of the house.

Two floors (the upper floors and the arch were added later) were at first occupied by the masters, and below, where I am now, was where the servants lived. That's obvious from the high ceilings of the upper floors, grand mantelpieces, and high windows. And in fact, I'm proud to call my apartment 'Basement,' even though it's nothing compared to the posh floors upstairs. Since they've erected a number of multistoried buildings on Barnov Street (I won't call them ugly because their owners probably love their apartments), the drains are absolutely useless, and every time it rains there's a smell of damp. I'm not happy about that, but what can I do? But I do know one thing, that as long as I am alive there will be no problems with the walls. They are very thick, built of bricks, and in some places filled with boulders from riverbanks. So they will certainly hold up.

It took me a long time to strip these walls, and perhaps if I had been more romantic and less lazy, I would probably have left samples of all the layers of old wall paper. There would have been at least ten, all different and silly. The ceiling in one small room had paintings too. You must have seen the like in the old houses of Tbilisi, especially where craftsmen lived, with birds and such, usually painted around the chandelier? In my room, there were painted daisies. But the painting was in a shambolic state, and for that reason I got rid of it. When I'm in a good mood, I'll paint new ones.

***

And now I'll tell you a different story. This one, too, is half-legend, a family legend this time. It recounts how it came about that I owned the lower floor of the Barnov House, not Rakovich nor Rikhalskaya.

It is thanks to my grandmother. Whenever I wake up in a good mood on Barnov Street, I call out, 'God love you, Granny Ana!' I can call it at the top of my voice, too, since the walls are so thick I won't frighten the neighbours.

At the time when money in the Soviet Union was totally useless, my granny was friendly with the former governor-general's lady-in-waiting, Olga Grigorievna Daniilova, who was the wife of the manager of the private office of the Chancellor of His Highness, Nikolai II. That honourable man was shot, as we well know, and Olga's daughter, Lyusa, escaped to London. To this day, no one knows whether she is dead or alive. To cut things short, that was a typical story of the time.

Right up until the end of her life, Madame Daniilova couldn't get used to her loss of status. She was hungry but she ate with a silver spoon. How could she possibly wear a cotton dress, she was not some kind of chamber maid! She chose her friends carefully too, and, as she used to say, she wasn't going to descend to being friendly with a load of bastards. I take these words as a compliment, because among the chosen were both my grandmother and the former owner of the house, Madame Rakovich-Dzigurova. Daniilova introduced these two women to each other. And when some dirty proletarian finally turned insolent and disputed Dzigurova's ownership of her house, my solicitor grandmother got involved in the dispute, and, imagine, she won the case. As you know, money wasn't money then, so the grateful Dzigurova decided to give a present to my grandmother and after much palaver she presented her with the following choice: she could either have a set of antique furniture, or the Barnov House. Granny chose the house, and praise be to God! What the hell would I have done with the furniture? Moreover, I have this wonderful chest of drawers, and Daniilova's iron bed. And as for the Barnov House, I love it, as much as I love my mother, father and probably my motherland.

TBILISI. NOVEMBER 2004

2nd November 2004

I have arrived. They weren't lying entirely. It is not cold, but the weather is somehow not the weather. But, on the other hand, what difference does it make to me, as if the weather in our country is any better. I simply expected the weather here to be different somehow.

I won't mention you in this new journal and I won't address any remarks to you either. That's decided. At least not while I'm here in Georgia. I'll think about it again once I'm gone. Perhaps, then, I won't have to write at all and I will be telling you everything face-to-face. Anyway, if I have told you everything already, I won't have lost anything, but I don't know. To put it in a nutshell, as I've told you, I will do my best, at least for now. But if I do address you, pay no attention, I'll simply rip out the page in question, so no one will ever find out.

Where I'm living, there's this woman, and I can't work out who she is. Either she's a housekeeper, or she lives here too, anyway I can't tell. She doesn't know any language that I can comprehend, nor am I able to make her understand anything when I speak. She swung my room door open without knocking and said, 'Pardon.' I smiled at her, because I thought she'd mixed up the rooms. Three minutes later, she came in again, once again without knocking, bringing along a small boy. The boy interpreted for her: he said that, because it was the first night I was spending under this roof, I had to put 'this' under my bed and make a wish, and my wish would come true. 'What should I put under my bed?' I asked. 'This,' he said, and took a small plate from the woman's hand. I could not understand what was going on, but the woman smiled at me. She had very strong, healthy teeth, and if anything happened, I reckoned she could bite my hand off. She said, 'Magic, magic,' and something else which the boy interpreted for me as 'good magic.'

Now, I don't know what to do with this plate. Is it good or bad? Magic is magic. I don't know. I couldn't understand that woman either, or make out what kind of woman she was, whether she was beautiful or ugly, whether I liked her or I didn't like her. But it must be some kind of magic, as she's made me write so much about this small plate.

And what wish do I want to come true? My exhibition or what? I decided that I would neither think about you nor write about you in my diary.

But what shall I think about?

3rd November 2004

I don't know whether I can attribute it to the plate, but one wish did come true. The sun appeared. From early morning someone was shouting outside, and later I was told that he was a yoghurt seller. In this district, they generally shout all the time—there are many street-sellers, rugs for sale, and a lot of bathhouses, with domes like hills. A bit further on, deep down in the district, Orthodox people come and go—men with long beards, and women in black headscarves—because there are a lot of churches concentrated here. There are art galleries here too, including ours, Karvasla, but there's also more of a sense of the Orthodox soul. I don't much like these men with their beards and women in their black headscarves. The men look at me directly, but the women don't look at me at all. None of them like me.

The wish that came true, thanks to the plate, didn't last long. It turned cold. It got dark early as they had put the clock back two days before. Neither I nor my local acquaintances could understand why they did that.

***

The food is delicious here, the only problem is that they use so many walnuts and spices that my liver will probably give up. I've already eaten three types of *khachapuri*. They eat *khachapuri*, this cheesy bread, all the time, and it comes in all kinds of varieties.

Today, in a big gallery on the main street, there was a photographic exhibition. They told me it was by Brits, but in fact the pictures were by Georgian, Armenian and Azerbaijani photographers. There were a lot of people milling about there, and I watched them instead of looking at the photos. Never mind, I'll go back tomorrow or the day after tomorrow, and I will see what kind of work these locals like.

Now Vato is taking me somewhere, to some artists' place. I'll probably be back late, so that's why I'm writing what ever I need to write now.

I don't have the plate anymore, nor have I seen that woman. Anyway, I'm now spending my second night here and her short-lived magic won't work anymore.

4th November 2004

The wine was very heavy. It tasted good, but in the morning my head was splitting. I couldn't possibly go to that photographic exhibition, I was in such a bad state. I don't feel especially lively now, nor do I care about my own exhibition much either.

Vato, though, feels quite alright. When I told him this morning that I was dying and that the woman gave me grappa to drink, he was highly amused.

Of course, that woman came in again without knocking on the door. She glanced at me, laughed, and left. Afterwards, that little boy brought me disgusting sweet coffee and some kind of thick, smelly liquid in an incredibly big crystal glass. This is grappa, the boy told me, and didn't take his eyes off me until I'd drunk to the bottom of the glass. Then he shouted something, and the woman replied from the corridor.

Then I fell asleep and slept as if I was dead until Vato arrived.

***

How nice that it's warm. We dealt with the exhibition too. There were a lot of people there, they seemed to enjoy the show, but what can you really tell? It is true that there are no real racial differences, that nationality is somewhat indefinable? and so on and so forth—the fact is that these people appear incomprehensible and weird to me, and a bit frightening. They speak far too loudly, as if they are always quarrelling. Georgian women's eyes are shrouded in darkness. Their eyes don't shine. Their faces are either totally motionless, like a stone, or else they are laughing loudly with their heads thrown back. I didn't observe the men a great deal, because they don't interest me that much, and also, it's generally agreed, they seem excessively aggressive.

You won't be reading this diary, but if you do, you will certainly be aware that, as a rule, I'm not afraid of people. How can anyone imagine that I might be afraid of these people? What nonsense! I simply avoid them.

5th November 2004

Once again, today I got involved in some stupid thing. No one's asked me, but this Georgian cuisine, mainly *khachapuri*, that cheesy bread, was getting a bit boring. For the first few days, it was fine, but now I'm not happy at all, having the same thing again and again. For the first few days, it was entertaining when they explained to me what it was. They also told me that when I ate it for the first time, I had to think of a wish and my wish would come true. I couldn't think of any wishes and soon I was no longer eating it for the first time. To cut a long story short, I was sick and tired of it.

I asked Vato, what do you do if you want to have coffee and cake? Thanks be to God that Vato's patriotic feelings are contained within sensible limits and he doesn't tend to get angry at silly things. I've been told that he's a member of a very old and famous aristocratic family here, that the members of this family were great public figures, and that there were monuments to some of them in Tbilisi. Vato doesn't show any aristocratic snobbism at all. It's easy to speak to him, and do things with him too. To put it in a nutshell, he's an ordinary man.

So, I asked Vato where I should go if I wanted coffee and cake and he told me to go to the Literature Café. I found myself on a very busy street, and for half an hour tried to cross the road. It was only later I noticed the underpass, but when I looked down it seemed filthy and there were no people around. I didn't go down there. What would be the point of getting myself killed in there?

There were a lot of people in the café, mainly women. One had her coffee cup on the piano for some reason, and an ashtray on the table. I sat at her table with my cake. The cake was nice.

Like everyone else, she interrogated me, asking where I came from, what I did, and in general what I wanted. The only thing she didn't ask me was whether or not I liked Georgia. She smoked and smoked, probably as many as ten cigarettes with one cup of coffee. Then they brought her tea, and she very unexpectedly took one of her shoes off, put her foot up on the chair and covered it with her dress. These Georgian women either wear the shortest dresses, so short that when they bend over you can see their underwear, or so long they get tangled up in the hem of their dress. Generally, their style of dress is a bit strange. I can't tell whether I like them or not. You can see soft hair on their stomachs beneath their short t-shirts, which could, in fact, be interesting, but I'm not so sure. My father always thinks of kidneys when he sees such outfits, but what can one say, he's an old man.

But here in Georgia, travelling in the minibuses, I see these hairy tummies and furry backs all the time, together with Gap lingerie. I wonder why Gap is so popular here. I must ask someone.

This woman wore a very long dress and, like most of the women in the café, she wore full evening make-up in the afternoon. She was wearing so much lipstick that it was visible on every cigarette butt in the ashtray. I like that very much, but I don't know how to talk to such a woman or what I'm supposed to do with her. But she spoke good English.

She shook the coffee cup and turned it over in a peculiar way, tilting it first from side to side and, after that, putting it upside down on the napkin, on top of the piano.

I asked her whether it was to indicate that she did not want any more coffee. She told me no, that's what they did in Turkey when they didn't want any more tea; she was doing it in order to tell a fortune. How would she do that? Easily, she replied, in the coffee grounds. She was going to look into her own cup to read her fortune for herself. Then she asked me if I could read her fortune. I told her that I couldn't and that I didn't believe in such things. She answered that I was foolishly mistaken. That's exactly what she said, and I felt completely nonplussed, because up to that point she didn't strike me as so badly brought up.

We sat in silence for a while, and then she told me that if I wanted, I could drink a cup of coffee and she would tell my fortune. Not from the cup I was drinking at that moment, but a different one, a Turkish coffee, and without waiting for my answer she spoke to the waitress and informed me that it would be brought straight away.

I told her that, here, everyone kept promising me that my wishes would come true and that I didn't know what to wish for. Anyway, I didn't know what I wanted. She told me that was nonsense. She'd been rude again, but what could I do? She told me that everybody had something they wanted, but that only some people dared to want something and some didn't. For example, she wanted lots of things, and, by the way, her wishes also came true. Her wishes always came true. And she lit a fresh cigarette.

I, too, felt like smoking a cigarette, and while I was searching my pockets, she took the cigarette out of her mouth and gave it to me. Just like that, like an old lover. A cigarette soiled with her lipstick. I accepted it, what else could I do? She told me that I had said that there was nothing I wanted and I had no wish, but really I wanted a cigarette, and when I expressed that, my wish came true.

I didn't quite follow her logic, but what could I do? I took the cigarette from her and started putting on my jacket. It was very awkward, because, as I was doing up the buttons, smoke was getting in my eyes, and for some reason I feel my eyes burning now. She asked me what I was doing. I told her I was leaving and thanked her for her wonderful company and the cigarette. She said that was okay and that she would drink my coffee.

Looking back, I think that that woman thought I was really foolish. You sometimes think I'm foolish too, don't you? I don't really know what I should do in such circumstances.

***

That woman sat there in such a manner it was clear she sits there all the time. And she must be local as they didn't object to her putting a coffee cup on the piano. Tomorrow I'll ask Vato to come there with me, and when I'm there with him, I'll be able to find out better what kind of woman she is.

There we are, I have a wish. That means it will come true.

6th November 2004
Today we are going to the ancient capital of Georgia. Apparently there are ancient cathedrals to see there. Vato said that, if we

managed to leave on time, he might take me to Stalin's Museum in Gori. It sounded interesting, but we definitely won't leave on time. I don't understand why they're always late, that's why I'm writing now. And we'll probably be back late this evening too, because a guy I met at Karvasla, the gallery, told me that we would have supper in a trendy restaurant in Mtskheta.

I won't drink any more wine. Georgian men drink vodka more, so perhaps they know this business better than me.

***

We didn't get to go to Gori, it would have gotten dark in three hours so it wasn't worth it. We went to the old capital and it was good, wonderful in fact. I was told a lot of history, only all of it was sad. Either a monk jumped into the river because he had fallen in love with a woman, or a very good king was buried under a mountain, or enemies used the cathedral in the mountains as stables.

I was told mostly about Saint Nino, and I liked those stories very much. It is true that I imagine her as completely different from how she is in the icons I see. In those she looks weak. I think that she must have been a very beautiful girl. She walked such distances on foot, but even so, the king wanted her as a wife. And it seems that she was also a very strong girl as she smashed various idols, and goodness knows what else she did or did not do. She was totally fearless.

In the convent there, the women were completely different. I can't stomach such women. Yes, I do like that they are dressed in black and dark colours, so you can't even tell whether they are young or old because you can't look into their faces. But I don't know what one can speak about to such women or what to do with them. Orthodox people in general are very different. When we were leaving, one of those women, perhaps she was a nun, came out and sat at the steering wheel of a white jeep. When I saw her I was astonished. She probably lights up a cigarette when she comes out of the gates, still all covered up and with that stern face. Wow, but one should probably not think about such things in the cathedral.

***

Although we left Mtkheta early we did not go to the Literature Café, I was tired and anyway I did drink wine after all as I found the vodka had a very bad taste. Never mind, I'll have a good night's sleep and after that I'll go to Karvasla.

So this woman said, just make a wish and it will come true. If that really was the case, I wouldn't have any problems.

***

When I come home, I so want not to have to sort anything out with you. I want very much not to flirt with you, but at the same time I want you to like me and I want you to be happy with me and to be proud of me, because I am so talented and so cool, and I want all the girls to be jealous because I am with you.

What stupid rubbish I'm writing. They definitely got me drunk. Never mind, I'll tear this page out tomorrow.

7th November 2004

Everyone is complimenting me on the exhibition. I'm pleased but I don't know whether they really think that or whether they are simply being polite. When they aren't addressing me directly they usually start speaking in Georgian. It's only Vato who is considerate. He avoids speaking any language I don't know in my presence, but no one else has such a good standard of English. So, usually, when they start speaking in Georgian, I always think they are talking about me and I get worried. If I told Vato that, he would probably laugh or think I'm paranoid, but I do worry. What can I do?

These days I spend all my time with the people from Karvasla and we constantly talk about art. They talk more than I do. They talk about the same things as artists do all over the world.

Artists are the same everywhere, wherever I have ever been. Most of them have spent a long time living in Europe, and goodness knows where else, and that's why they don't differ a great deal from each other, apart from their appearance and their languages. It's hard to know whether some of them are so hard up that they genuinely can't afford to get their teeth fixed, or whether that's just a pose they adopt. But one particular artist's teeth really shocked me. I was horrified, he was such a young man and it seemed he had no pride. I'd think the same thing even if he were old. However, he was accompanied by a cute young girl. I wonder how that cute girl can bear to kiss him. Perhaps she has something wrong with her too, gum disease or something similar. Yuck.

This girl told me that, some time ago, a pigeon flew into her window. Then her friend had a dream that that girl herself owned a bird, multi-coloured and smooth, with a neat, pointed beak, and after that the toothless man gave her a painting and the painting was of a bird. 'And what happened then?' I asked. 'Then I got acquainted with a foreign bird. You!' she said and roared with laughter. She doesn't appear to have any signs of gum disease, but really, she isn't quite all there.

I'm not fit to go to the Literature Café today either. This evening, we're going to visit some photographer. I've seen his pictures and they look wonderful, but I've yet to meet the man himself. The guys said he usually has an excellent grappa. That means I will get drunk again, and tomorrow I'll have a splitting headache.

I wonder where that woman of mine disappeared to? If I have a splitting headache again tomorrow, I hope she'll bring grappa.

I'll probably become an alcoholic.

***

I can't sleep. At first I did fall asleep, but now I've woken up and have a terrible headache. First, I thought I would write about Gurami's, but there's no way I'm up to it. My head is throbbing.

I've read my previous writings and I won't tear out any of the pages. Why should I rip them out? You won't read them anyway. You couldn't give a toss, could you?

8th November 2004

I think I must be in love with that neighbour of mine, or else I don't know what the hell is going on, well, anyway, I'm in love with that woman. When I woke up, I waited like an idiot for the moment she would barge into my room.

When she came in, I laughed, and she laughed too. It seems to me that there must be some people waiting in front of the house in order to tell her when I've come home drunk. I should keep a look out. But if you ask me, I don't stagger, and if I'm drunk it doesn't show at all.

This time she brought mineral water instead of grappa and that was good too. I still have the taste of Gurami's grappa in my mouth, but still that water was really good. While I was drinking it, she wandered round the room. I was afraid that she might open the curtains, the sunshine would have driven me mad, but she didn't. She's probably been taking care of drunks all her life.

'Finish?'

I replied, 'Finish.' She left.

There was no running water in the tap. There's still no water. Now I understand what that heavy smell is in the minibuses. Never mind, I'll ask Vato and he will do something about it.

***

I went to the bathhouse. From now on I'll go there every day. Why did I bother to splash around in that bathroom the size of a cupboard? Afterwards we went up the hill somewhere, there were domes there too, and we drank tea in some very dilapidated tea rooms. The weather is nice again.

I wish it didn't get dark so early. When it's dark I feel too lazy to go to the Literature Café, otherwise I would have gone there and invited that woman to the tea rooms. I'm sure she's never been there. Such well-groomed and highly made-up women probably don't go to such places.

It makes no sense to invite the woman next door. We can't converse, and also she would know those tea rooms better than I do.

I so want to invite someone out somewhere, because my life is just business, business, all the time. It's nice in the evenings. It's good anyway, but it's still better not to have business all the time. To speak about business and yet more business. I have enough of that at home.

The guys told me that there are prostitutes working near the domes of the big new bathhouse. As they said it, they were laughing kind of lewdly, and I started laughing in the same way.

I felt like getting some sex, too. I'm an idiot. Thank goodness that you will never read this writing. But if you did read it ... I don't know.

What am I trying to do—make you jealous? What a nuisance.

9th November 2004

I was at Gurami's today again. Gurami doesn't know English and he tried to explain something in German, but I didn't understand anything he said. There were two more photographers at his house—women, Lisa and Ira. I realised that they weren't Georgian. There was an exhibition of work by those two girls at the British exhibition that day and I felt ashamed that I couldn't find anything to say about it. I don't remember a single photo and I don't remember them either.

I wish I'd met these girls earlier. They are full of life, and interesting. Lisa is big and fair-haired, she laughs loudly, and she is not at all shy. They spoke Russian and Lisa laughed all the time. Gurami has a photo of her standing near the staircase. It's one of a series he's made where he took pictures of people wearing masks. In the photograph, Lisa has black lips and a huge tongue sticking out of her mouth. It's a cool photo and Lisa is a cool girl too. She doesn't touch a drop of alcohol but nevertheless she laughs all the time.

Ira looks more like a model than a photographer, but Gurami said that she was a good photographer. I didn't see a photograph of Ira in a mask. She has long, straw-coloured hair and green eyes, but her skin is dark. She's cheerful too, but she laughs quietly. While I was there, she quietly sat in the corner and smiled. She talked to me, saying that she'd seen my work and liked it, but that means nothing. I realise that now, because everybody says the same about the photos.

Gurami's bedroom is on the second floor. I don't remember anymore why I went up there, perhaps it was to phone someone, but thank God I did. On the wall, there's such a photo, my jaw dropped. The photo is great but the model is something else. She is a bit like you, but because you will not bother to read this, I can say without any fear, that she is much more beautiful than you. 'Do you like her?' Ira shouted from below. 'Very much,' I said, and Liza laughed loudly, only I could not understand what she was laughing at. I hope she wasn't laughing at me. She would not have mocked me, she doesn't seem to be nasty like that. Ira told me that the girl did not live in Tbilisi, she apparently went to Europe, where some trendy photographers were photographing her. She'd apparently been a model for Liza, Gurami and Ira. They praised her a lot, but it's not relevant any more.

Then Gurami had to go somewhere and Lisa, Ira and I went together to the Literature Café. Everything was completely different with them, we laughed all the time, we chose different cakes and shared them with each other. That woman wasn't sitting near the piano, she didn't appear at all. Now, in the evening, everything was different, the women's make-up wasn't so obvious either. It was good that I went back there once again, and that the first visit won't haunt me like some kind of bad dream.

I asked the girls whether they told fortunes. They said they did sometimes. 'Do your wishes come true?'

'Pretty much,' they said.

In this country, no matter who you ask, everyone says that everything will be alright and wishes will all come true. 'We will be very happy,' they say. They don't look as if that's the case. I don't understand either how they live or where they get their money from, or how they manage any enthusiasm for life. There are constant wars, or elections, they curse politicians the whole time, beggars are always running in the streets, they nearly jump under the cars, you only need to see photographs. It's totally depressing, but still they are always happy, having fun—not like Americans. It seems to me they really do enjoy life. It seems the wishes they have must be different and they always come true. For example, that woman at the piano the other day, if they want a cigarette and somebody gives them one, or, I don't know, something along those lines, that can make them happy.

Well, it could be because of the climate. It's always sunny and warm. And that's already something positive.

10th November 2004

I think I have the flu. I've got a sore throat and my ear is blocked, and in general I don't feel well at all, perhaps they infected me. I'm very fed up.

Vato told me that going to the bathhouse can help with such

illnesses. So I went to the bathhouse—not to the individual compartments, but into the communal area. I was there for ages. That masseur or washer or whatever he was called, worked so hard on me, I was exhausted. In fact, I'll never go there again. It was full of hairy men, some of them with such bellies that your heart stops in terror, and, besides, everyone tries to speak to you, but they can't, and the floor was filthy too.

But I was thoroughly warmed up and when I got home, I was no longer ill. I was just completely exhausted. Vato said that it was okay and that I could rest all day long, and that they would tell me later what they had talked about at their meeting. That's why I went to a mini-market and asked a woman shop assistant to give me some grappa. She couldn't understand anything I said and called somebody else. She didn't understand anything either, and then I realised they didn't know what grappa was. But they knew vodka and I bought a small bottle.

At home I drank this vodka and, after that, a very large cup of a very hot and sweet tea. I squeezed a lot of lemon juice into it too. Vato taught me that. After that I took some pills and fell asleep. It was still sunny but it would have got dark soon.

Then, about three hours later, I woke up and since then I have been wide awake. I have a sore throat again and now both ears are blocked. What's wrong with me?

***

I had just managed to get to the exhibition before closing time, and for that reason there wasn't time to see it properly. There was furniture from some famous Georgian designer. The man himself was there but his English was not very good, so we couldn't talk a lot.

I thought I would meet Ira and Lisa at the exhibition as they said they were coming, but they were not there, perhaps I'd missed them. I couldn't ask that man, the designer, as perhaps he does not know who they are. Even so, I went to the Literature Café afterwards, but they weren't there either. Some men were lording it over the place as if they were kings, and my made-up girls were dotted around. The piano woman wasn't anywhere to be seen. To put it in a nutshell, it was a bad day.

Now I'm lying in bed once more and I don't know what to do. I feel sleepy again. I will phone Vato now and tell him that I am fine and that I will go to Karvasla tomorrow morning. I will take some medication and that will be that.

I wish I had taken Lisa's or Ira's phone numbers. But in any case, they didn't ask for mine either. Probably they don't want to meet me.

I wonder whether you ever really liked me. I also wonder whether, if I had started a relationship with this 'piano' woman, I would be thinking about you?

What kind of relationship could have come out of that encounter if I don't even remember the woman's face?

11th November 2004

I can't make out what kind of art these people like. Or even what kind of people they are. If they are like Gurami, why do they attend such a horrible exhibition as the one I went to today? Exactly the same people go to exactly the same places. I recognize their faces, and they go everywhere wearing the same expression. I really can't grasp what kind of people they are. They are middle-aged, they are definitely not teenagers, they seem to be educated and erudite, and at the same time they seem to be critical. They don't have any money but they still spend all their time sitting in that expensive café, the one near Karvasla. The women wear second-hand clothes but they smell of the latest perfumes. How wonderful that you taught me how to distinguish perfumes. At least I learned something useful from being with you.

One such arty person or, I don't know, let's say an art lover, or something, spoke to me for a long time, and told me that he had been to my homeland, that he had skied in winter and that there were some really fine lakes in my country. Apparently he had been to Switzerland. I didn't laugh or get annoyed, what does he matter to me anyway?

After the exhibition we went to that snobbish café. There's a new sculpture in the street, of the film director, Parajanov, who was Georgian, more precisely, Armenian, but a native of Tbilisi. I liked the sculpture, but that art person, or connoisseur of art, the one who had been to Switzerland, said that it looked like Karls-son-on-the-roof—a portly character in a Russian kids' cartoon, and he winked at me. I asked, 'Why Karlsson-on-the-roof—because it can fly?' I like the sculpture very much.

I'm probably really sick. Everything got on my nerves all day long. In that café, I completely lost the plot. There were some scented candles there and there were also some beautiful women, but they had mobiles in their hands, or were smoking in a deep thoughtful manner with half-closed eyes. I asked one of the women at our table, who looked a bit more lively, whether she could look into my cup and tell my fortune. She roared with laughter.

Vato didn't join us. Perhaps I'm not completely crazy, that really wasn't a very good place.

In the evening, I decided to walk in the Old City. At first, everything was fine, but I didn't dare to go to the upper streets, they were very dark and there was nobody to be heard or seen there. Never mind, I'll go there tomorrow, or the day after tomorrow. I am here for one more week.

***

If I don't write this down, I'll completely lose my mind. I was going so crazy that I nearly phoned Vato to tell him about it, but then I realised that it would take a lot of time.

I was just about to fall asleep when somebody started rattling the door handle and banging so hard on the door that I nearly had a heart attack. I asked who was there and a woman's voice answered. She seemed to be angry.

I got up, put on my clothes and opened the door. All this time she had been knocking on the door and driving me mad. When I opened it, there was that neighbour woman. As God's my witness, I wasn't seeing things, she actually had a coffee cup in her hand.

She entered as if I had been begging her to come in all my life. She put a cup on the top of the chest of drawers, and gestured with her eyes for me to go back inside the room. I nodded towards the clock to show her it was nearly midnight. She shook her head as if she did not understand.

I drank that coffee. It was already cool so I swallowed it quickly. She didn't allow me to have the last gulp but grabbed the cup from my hand. These Georgian women take liberties, and just like that piano woman did, she rolled it from one side to the other. Then she poured the liquid onto the saucer and threw the cup straight onto the invitation card to my exhibition. I nearly shouted at her, but what sense would that have made? She banged my shoulder with her hand, not at all lightly, and went out. She left the door open so I guessed that she would come back.

This time, instead of the small boy, she brought with her a plump, bottle-blonde with plucked eyebrows, who was wearing leather trousers. She was very amusing. She had a piece of chewing gum stuck on her ring, and when she finished drinking her coffee, she popped the chewing gum back in her mouth. This girl knew nice English, and she asked me questions about everything, very clearly, even questioned my beliefs. Both of them sat on my bed, the yellow-haired one was doing the talking whilst the other one was deep in thought, looking into my cup. Then she started to speak and the bottle-blonde interpreted.

She told me that I had not understood anything and that I had travelled a long road in order to understand, but nevertheless, I understood nothing. She talked to me about you too, she said that you were not as I wanted you to be, that you were much more, and that was the reason why nothing worked with you. Suddenly she got angry and told me that I took too many liberties, and that until I thought about you as much as myself, I didn't deserve to get anywhere, that my work or whatever I did would be without any commitment. She told me that you didn't need any abstract idea of loyalty and that thinking about you wasn't enough. You needed me to have no secrets from you anymore, and so on. She turned the cup in a theatrical manner and held it out under my nose. Nothing could be hidden in this cup.

Then she told me that I had a long road ahead, probably leading home, and also a short one. It might seem insignificant, but this short road would bring me great joy and I would have a second chance to understand something. 'What do I need to understand?' I asked her. 'You know what,' she told me. Then she told me that I had already had success and that I would have more. But that my next success would be in a different business from the one I was engaged in at the moment. She told me that after I'd travelled that long road in my life, a woman from the past, whom I'd almost forgotten forever, would return, unexpectedly, for a short time, 'and you will think that you've returned home.' 'What woman?' She shrugged her shoulders. She told me to make a wish now and put my finger into the coffee grounds.

Again a wish! What should I wish? Anyway, this coffee business is so stupid! I couldn't think of any wish at all, and poked my finger into the cup. She looked into it and smeared her finger in there too.

'Nothing comes from nothing,' the bottle-blonde interpreted.

'I told you already that you understood nothing!'

Then they left. The one with yellow hair wished me good night.

I am rather afraid of that bad-mannered woman. If it were daytime it would have been okay. I will try to come home late tomorrow, or perhaps not at all, perhaps I'll stay at Vato's, or ask Lisa and Ira to come to my place for the night. It's nothing to do with sex, we'll just laugh together.

12ᵗʰ November 2004

The town above my house was looking beautiful. It's a lovely autumn, very warm. If I start to describe it, I'll sound sweet and sentimental, but that's really what it was like, so what can I do?

Now, I'm sitting in a café, in the new part of the city, a long way from the streets where I usually make my journeys. This is also a literary café, but very different. Downstairs, a young lecturer has invited four enthusiastic students for coffee and I could make out that they were discussing Kafka, but as soon as there was a free seat upstairs, I moved here. From here, I can see the street better and it's easier to catch the attention of a waiter.

I have the whole table to myself, that's why I can write easily. There's a young man in front of me. He looks like a terrorist and is sitting and drinking tea, and reading something with great interest. Such men are probably attractive to our women because they are so dark. That big dog apparently belongs to the man too. The dog is well-behaved and is looking out of the window like a human being, and only once jumped up at some girls. They knew it and weren't frightened, but even so, the man reprimanded it, and the dog went back to the window.

Today is a good day.

Some young girls, probably students, have barged in. Five girls sat at one table and ordered just two glasses of juice. The poor café owner! No, look, here they're bringing coffee too. They will drink it, roll the grounds around and tell each other thousands of foolish things.

If I had days like this all my life, I wouldn't be able to achieve anything. I would sit and sit like this, in front of the big window.

Look at these youngsters. They are staring meaningfully either at this terrorist or at me. The terrorist does not look at them at all, he turns the pages of his book, but as for me, it goes to my head. If he were in our country, our girls would go to his head too, that's for sure.

Well, of course, they asked me for a light. I will write something now so that they think that I'm really writing something, and then I will move to a different seat.

13th November 2004

Yesterday, I was in a Tbilisi night club which, for some reason, is called Berlin. It must have been some industrial building once as it is a huge space. We arrived very late, about one a.m. I was drunk and that's why I don't know what kind of girls my companions were. They were probably drunk too.

I didn't think about you at all yesterday. Today, I don't have a headache and I will go to Vato's now, I will tell him yesterday's news and then, in the evening, Vato has invited me and Tiniko to San Sushi, not to the palace but to the café.

Had I lost my mind? What kind of joke was this San Sushi?

***

Tiniko told me that she knew a bit of Swedish. Once upon a time, a man taught her. 'He's a publisher now. Do you want me to introduce you to him?' 'What for?' I asked. 'In order to speak Swedish to him,' she said.

I don't want to meet a Swedish-speaking publisher, nor to speak Swedish. Nor do I want Tiniko to speak Swedish, and anyway, I want nothing. I was very happy to learn that Tiniko lived some distance away and that's why she had to go home by taxi and I paid for her taxi too. She left. Today, I think nothing has made me as happy as this.

I can bear anything for three days, even Tbilisi. I'm not happy at the thought of going home or sorting out my relationship with you.

The cats are yowling under my window. What a time for a cats' wedding! In this country, the cats are off their heads, just like the human beings. They don't know what season it is, they shout and yowl and behave like they are stupid.

If that woman opens my door now I will go mad. I'll lock it and switch off the lights as well, and then perhaps I will be safe.

But, on the other hand, I wish she would come in. I will tell her everything, what I think about her and those like her. She doesn't know English, but I would make her understand.

14th November 2004

People in Parnas Café have been drinking since midday. That terrorist guy only drank tea. All the girls greeted him and he behaved exceptionally well towards everyone. He smiled at them and spoke to them cordially. He wasn't accompanied by the dog today and he had put a wheelie bag against the wall. The terrorist's face, military trousers, beautiful girls, and one wheelie bag. If he comes again tomorrow, I'll take his picture.

Some women looked at me and gave me an invitation to some gallery. I won't go but I put it in my pocket anyway, to be polite.

Today, in Parnas, I listened to the political discussion for the first time. To be precise, it was a monologue, or a meeting, I don't know. If I understand anything at all, then it was definitely political. There were three guys sitting at the table: a red-haired guy, one with glasses, one big boy, and then one woman of an uncertain age. She was dressed in what you would call a unisex style, only she had wavy and tousled hair, and silver rings on each finger. To put it briefly, she was certainly a woman. At first, they spoke among themselves, and then they spoke to that terrorist, and then one more woman joined them. She looked like several old gold coins, with her gold hair and yellow coat. She was a beautiful woman and she had long fingers. When she sat down, she tucked her dress, which had been flapping around her ankles, between her inner thighs, and I saw that she had such legs that she should have walked without a dress all the time. So, that woman joined them and then all hell broke out.

Unisex was getting very heated. She seemed to be an eloquent speaker. She was speaking in long sentences and from time to time made some obscene gestures. In fact, she was talking about fucking somebody. I thought she was a feminist. I got very interested in what was going on. It wasn't my business but I had to do something. I will definitely bring my camera tomorrow, and perhaps they will be there again.

It was all fascinating stuff. After a while I guessed that they were talking about Chechnya. The women and the white-haired one were insisting on one thing, and the one with the glasses, something else. The terrorist clearly could hear everything, and I think he was on the women's side too. He didn't get involved himself, only the golden-haired one would gesture towards him from time to time. She definitely used him as a witness. I wonder whether that terrorist was Chechen.

Then Unisex lost the plot and started shouting 'fascist' all the time. I thought that soon she would shout out some anthem, and believe it or not, she really did sing. I don't know what it was, but I know that it was definitely an anthem, I had heard it somewhere, but I don't remember where. The gold-haired one even clapped her hands in time to the rhythm. Unisex didn't have a brilliant voice, but she sang with all her heart, and, to my surprise, the one in glasses joined in with her.

I wished Vato had been there. He would at least have explained to me what was going on. As a rule, because beautiful women can speak English, it's likely that Beauty would have known it, but I could hardly ask her to interpret for me what they were shouting about, could I?

But Georgians are bad-mannered people. Why are they shouting? I can imagine how it must have been here last year during the revolution. How they would have shouted! It's amazing they didn't kill each other. But then what? They shouted, shouted some more, and then they ordered vodka. They banged their glasses together and, afterwards, drank water from one glass. I have the feeling that everything is a show. I already realised that all this making of toasts is a show. They are amusing themselves. When we were in that nightclub, Berlin, no one proposed any toast, although we drank a lot. Neither Vato nor his friends ever make toasts, because they do something meaningful. They are thinking people, so they don't have time left for saying silly things.

As a rule, neither Unisex nor her beautiful friend should have been idle. The golden-haired one had a huge bag next to her. I wonder how she lugs it around, and Unisex had her mobile ringing every few minutes. It is true that she kept switching it off, as she couldn't deal with it, but nevertheless they phoned her. That means that somebody needed her for something and she must be a doer of something. Well, even I could guess that suitors would not be phoning her. What would you say to such a woman or what could you do with such a woman? I prefer you to such women too—at least I know for sure that I'm dealing with a woman, whether she's good or bad.

15th November 2004
In this town, all the books I come across in bookshops were designed by Gurami. He also designs the cover of the English-

language magazine about Georgian literature. I bought a small book about him with his own illustrations. I'll definitely show it to you when I get back.

How awful, I really am coming back soon. I thought that the visit to Tbilisi would give me something. Well, it has given me something. I will be able to write on my CV, 'participation in Georgian-Swedish project.' I have seen a new country that I didn't know, I met some people. I will do a lot of things with Vato in the future. I will have some tales to tell at home too. What more have I thought about? Nothing at all. I wasn't here looking for either a great love or eternal blessing of the soul. There are lots of countries like this in the world and I can live without Georgian polyphonic harmony and *khachapuri* too.

But, even so, I am sorry to be leaving. So what exactly am I sorry about?

We were visiting an acquaintance of Vato's in the Old City. Her place was a huge apartment, quite shabby, but still grand. The walls were covered with everything you can imagine: a rug, a misty mirror in its frame with angels and roses, big paintings, everywhere angels and roses in the same type of frames. As a rule, it should have been maddening, but it was actually very good. Even now I wonder why. At one stage I thought that I hated such houses, because I did not have one like that, and in reality I wanted one. But I don't think so. If I did have one, I would have sold the angels and roses at once and redecorated. And so it would not be the same house.

In order to make me lose my mind completely there was a lampshade over the round table, the tablecloth was white with white embroidery, and they served us sweet biscuits with the tea. The cat walked to and fro, although it did not behave insolently like all other Georgian cats. It didn't jump on me or sharpen its claws on my trousers.

The host had been a painter at some point. Now, apparently,

she was involved in some way with the diplomatic service. She was a woman of thirty or thirty-five and she had something to discuss with Vato. I didn't ask what and she did not talk much with Vato either. We stayed for a while, we drank some tea, and that was that. When we were leaving, she saw us off and then went to the shop, and while we tried to hail a taxi, she came out of the shop with a big bottle of vodka. I asked Vato whether she drank. 'Didn't you even realise that she was already drunk?' he said.

Well, it seems that I really don't understand anything, and never will either. She lives in such a house, she has such work, and yet she drinks? And alone and in the daytime? She did not offer us any vodka.

16th November 2004

How amazing, I'm leaving tomorrow. That was all in all just two weeks. I'm writing this diary for the last time. I will write now, then put it in my bag so that I'm not running around like a headless chicken tomorrow looking for it.

What I'm reading, though, is nothing to be happy about. Nothing has happened during all this time and I have not written anything. I have not written anything about the exhibition either, nor about you. And in general, it's as if I forgot about the exhibition. And when I wrote at the beginning that I would not mention you, that was nonsense, how can I not mention you? Who should I mention then?

But I thought I would not mention that woman, and how, in the afternoon, nothing happened. All in all, it's idiotic stuff, but what stuff is ever clever? To be brief, when I bought wine, as a present for you by the way, my dear, on the narrow street near the big bathhouse, the woman in a dress was standing there and she was washing a rug. She spread it in the middle of the street and was spraying it with cold water from a hose pipe. She had raised the hem of her dress to the waist and she was vigorously scrubbing the rug with a brush. She didn't hear my footsteps, but when I passed her she looked up and raised the middle finger of her free left hand. She laughed at me too. She had big, healthy teeth.

I hope the wine will be good. Vato told me that I should buy *chacha*, Georgian grappa, but they didn't have it in the mini-market, and I was too lazy to go and look for it anywhere. Moreover, today is my last day and I have got lots of things to do.

WHEN A PARROT FLIES OVER YOU

My dear! The story I want to tell you began long ago, in the jaw-dropping Sixties of the last century, but not like you think, with flowers in the hair and rock 'n' roll, but with one disgusting trial. The man against whom there was a lawsuit wasn't a good man at all.

Imagine a man with two previous convictions. It wasn't enough for someone called Caryl Chessman to commit armed robbery, he also raped several women at the scene of the crime. Of course, such behaviour can't be considered heroic and the sentence of execution, according to Californian State Law, wasn't a surprise. During the twelve years he spent in prison, Chessman fought vigorously to save his life and prove the truth. This over-the-top, eccentric, and, according to some people, pathological behaviour, became the subject of a disagreement between two generations—parents and their children.

The fact that his pathological behaviour could have been the driving force of the social revolution was unimaginable for the generation of fathers who once fought against unemployment, were ready to sacrifice their lives for Spain, and were opposed to Hitler's ideology. And of course, veterans of the Korean War, and the Second World War, with their short haircuts, had heart attacks when their children suddenly shouted their demands for free love, accompanied by the songs of a new troubadour with scruffy hair and a hoarse voice, a Jew from Hibbing, Minnesota, a certain Robert Zimmerman. Their children rushed on to the streets, demanding that that villain, Caryl Chessman, should be released.

Yes, before that, in 1958, one day in Alabama State, a black woman—you see how politically correct I am, I didn't say Negro, did I?—anyway, this woman, her name was Rosa Parks, got on a bus and sat on the front seat. She was very tired and didn't remember that she was Negro and didn't have the right to sit there at the front of the bus. This act, at first glance, seems insignificant, but Madame Rosa aroused the black civil rights movement, which was dormant, but already at the point of awakening, along with Dr Martin Luther King, Jr.". It's precisely thanks to her that today we are not ashamed to have white skin.

Besides, in 1959, a very handsome, young and daring son of wealthy Cubans, together with his victorious band of revolutionaries, in other words, with many healthy, bearded men, came down from the Sierra Maestra and ousted Batista. And what a guy that Che Guevara was, daring to light such a revolutionary fire just eighty miles away from the States! Whether you approve of his behaviour or not is a separate issue, but there's no arguing with me that Che is a sex symbol.

It was against this background of the events I've just described, as well as many others, that the new generation decided to start everything again from scratch, and unleashed their own revolution. (Some of the things I described may seem foolish to you from today's point of view, and yet you're delighted by this bit of my letter, which, at first sight, has nothing to do with the main topic—that is to say, sex.) Their revolution, as most revolutions usually are, was inspired by idealistic desires, and led to the sacrifice of multiple victims.

Afterwards, these revolutionaries, like other revolutionaries, turned into a peaceful and business-like bourgeoisie, although if you ask me, they became bastards. But to analyse that is neither my business nor the subject of your interest. I told you all these stories in order to remind you how everything began. The so-called sexual revolution, if there's any justice, should have touched us too. After so many wars, hell, and trouble, we should have at least guessed that love is better than war—love, peace, freedom, and happiness.

But it seems we've failed to understand that. I don't know why. We are either stupid or extremely frightened. Sometimes we're afraid of society, sometimes of God, sometimes of AIDS, and sometimes, and most often this—that if it finishes, ouch, if it finishes, 'no one would not never love us.'

Three rejections, a triple negative, what the hell is that?

***

I've visited many cities during my short, but fortunately very varied, life and that's probably why I have discovered one very curious characteristic of my hometown. Here men and women don't kiss each other. One supposes they must kiss somewhere, I don't know, behind a door that's been bolted nine times, or in dark parks, but the scenes I so enjoy watching in other places can't be seen anywhere in Tbilisi, that's to say, couples who love each other. I don't know whether they love each other for eternity or only momentarily, but it is a fact that they are happy together at that point in time. If nothing else, at least to see couples embracing each other gives hope that such joy might sometime come to me. But, no! In Tbilisi, only drunk men kiss each other, or very young female friends, and then it's clear that when girls kiss each other, they don't feel overjoyed about anything and will probably never feel delighted with anything. The worst thing, as far as I'm concerned, is to observe mothers licking their offspring. To describe this dead kiss, Tbilisi teenagers have invented a funny abbreviation. They switch on their mobiles and send a short text message—MWA!—to each other, and I feel sick.

But I remember a wave which went round the world before my birth and which, fortunately for me, reached Georgia when I was old enough to understand its implications. Someone called it the 'Sexual Revolution,' someone else, the 'Blossom Time for the Children of Flower Power.' Somebody else called it the 'Porno-Political Movement,' and this last name is entirely outrageous. One way or another, I remember that, during Soviet times, we had so-called non-Soviet days, such as the celebration of St Casimir's Day and one-night stands. I remember there was a big revolution involving rucksacks. Thousands, perhaps millions, of young people have rucksacks on their backs. They go up the mountains to pray, children laugh, old people are pleased, young girls are happy, and slightly older girls are even happier. They are mad about Zen, they write poems that suddenly pop into their minds, and because they are compassionate, because their actions are mysterious and unexpected, a vision of glorious freedom opens up in each human being and every living creature. It is true that Jack Kerouac wrote about Americans, whom I'd only seen in the movies at that time, and politically this writer should also have been anathema to me. As far as I was concerned, he was an ultra-reactionary, he was full of hatred for the New Left, but what can I do, no one managed to describe those events better than he did.

I will try to explain. Sexual freedom for me is equivalent to the struggle against the establishment, censorship and war. Any fight against a false society begins with a fight against its false ethical standards. 'The main thing is to grab its genitals, the brain and soul won't run away anywhere.'

And now, when we don't have to pursue non-Soviet days, and nobody prohibits us from doing anything, and when there are lots of nice things going on in our warm city, for some reason we get angry a lot, because, imagine, the Hungarian painter, Mihály Zichy was a pornographer! They still think that the curse, 'fuck your mother' refers to sex, woman are reminded of 'their past,' and they say that using condoms is the same as genocide. What's happening with us? And, as I mentioned above, no one kisses each other. Either we're embarrassed, or we don't want to kiss, or, and it's sad but perfectly possible, it's simply that no one loves anyone.

***

Have you heard of the Hindu god, Kama? He is a very strange god. He's god of love, not love of a neighbour, or a friend, or the motherland, but of erotic love. He rides on a parrot and flies everywhere, even where other gods have no business to be. No one can oppose Kama, and that's a good thing, otherwise our lives would have been extremely dull and we would have never been able to truly be in the here and now—instead spending all our time uselessly remembering the past or making pointless plans for the future.

When Kama's colourful bird flies somewhere else alone, we burden our minds with thousands of silly things. We think that those who own more are happier, and those who produce more are more influential. We believe that everybody should belong to the majority. They should identify themselves with the majority and drink Coca-Cola, and that there's something wrong with those who don't feel happy all the time. But believe me: happiness, that total all-encompassing joy, is only brought by Kama, in other words by erotic love, and, of course, the love which is not suppressed or secret, but which is fulfilled; the kind of love which fills the soul with joy.

Knowledgeable people say that the main thing is apparently to be loyal to Kama, in other words, to be loyal to love. In this case, it doesn't matter whether this love is directed at one person or that you have many objects of desire. Kama isn't interested. Kama is only interested in loyalty to love. It is important for Kama that we are loyal to love. When a human being lives with another without love, whether man or woman, and if he or she cohabits 'only because,' they are committing a sin against Kama, against love, and love, as you know, is God. You can call it anything you like, but for me, it is called Kama.

But you have probably noticed, too, that the passionate love of Kama is looked at with some degree of irritation. For some reason sex is considered problematic, and we have to do everything to follow behavioural norms set by somebody else, and to keep it secret, to speak about it ironically, to suppress it, and afterwards, for some reason, we are surprised that Kama, who is offended and somewhat insulted, abandons us and goes to people who have more open hearts.

The universe changes colour without Kama. We change too, and afterwards, because emptiness is a very unnatural state, a lot of ugliness nestles in our hearts instead of colourful Kama. Do you remember Reich's theory? That suppressed sex gives rise to dictators. Do we want dictators? I think not.

So, let's look around and listen, and merciful, joyful Kama will certainly fly towards us, and we will be happy, in the here and now.

That was some kind of romantic deviation, so that you don't think that this woman (in other words me, A.K.S.) is appealing to you to engage in immoral behaviour and pushing us into a whirlpool of depravity. What are you talking about? I just wanted to say that freedom, a word which we've worn out so much that even the notion itself doesn't make our hearts beat faster, definitely implies the freedom of feelings, or, if you like, sexual freedom. If that's not the case, I think that the struggle for sexual freedom, even the very word combination, is foolish in itself. Why is it necessary to struggle? Sex is natural. So, any kind of wish to suppress it is unnatural. Sex isn't perverted at all; it is perverted of society to consider it as such. Society considers that bliss perverted—that one that everyone strives for. Even a decent citizen with his tie done up tightly and his permanently unhappy life-companion succumb to this bliss. And anti-social elements of society, considered unacceptable by this decent couple, should also succumb to it. The difference is only that these anti-social elements greatly enjoy sex, while this respectable couple considers sex reprehensible. They keep it thoroughly hidden, they even hide it from each other, and, as a result, instead of experiencing joy, they perhaps get a somewhat dubious pleasure. That's why the man runs off to an expensive brothel to be with the cheap whores, and his wife gets old and fat.

They have decided that social status, being comfortable, and having thousands of formalities, are worth more than love. They don't love each other and they don't wish to, but I think that there is no difference between loveless cohabitation without any desire and rape. I will never understand why this form of rape is accepted by society. If you can't honestly tell the person you are embracing for those few seconds that you love them very much, it is better not to approach them at all. Such a union will result in disillusion, and hopelessness instead of ecstasy, and will bring feelings of dirtiness. Apparently, Kama, the god of love, punishes traitors.

It's very difficult to imagine that two people can find each other immediately in the following way. Kama flew over and two individuals, who previously hadn't experienced any passion, bumped into each other, and, ever since, they have been loving each other and have lived happily together for a long time, until one day they die simultaneously. Such things, I'm afraid, only happen in books, but in real life everything is different. There is delight, excitement, and madness, which an inexperienced creature, male or female, calls love, and then everything ends, if they are lucky, quickly. If they aren't lucky, they torture each other for a time that lasts much longer than the earlier period of love and excitement, and the wonderful dream, which was wonderful precisely because it originated as love, turns into a nightmare. One wise friend explained to me, 'Love is a breeze which blows in from an open window. If you try to capture it by shutting the window, it will immediately disappear.' If you don't believe him or me, try it for yourself.

And it's difficult to say what the difference is between love and sex. 'I love you, but I don't want you,'—who has heard such a thing? When it concerns one object, both sex and love are temporary. I can't believe that a person never felt burning desire for another, even when they are with their unique, incomparable beloved. The thing which was called the sexual revolution, what kind of revolution was it? Sex is sex, it has always been like that—wonderful—what is new about it now? It did bring one big advantage—it brought experience. You may have a lot of partners, but you can have only one love. They say that happiness is the destiny of the chosen few, or a result of tremendous effort. To experience sweetness and bitterness, joy and pain, rising and falling, heaven and hell, is really a passionate and sublime thing, is it not? A human being will eventually learn to find a point of balance and understand that the end of the honeymoon is the beginning of love, and when the flash of passion burns out, the celebration of the soul begins. I have to tell you that I've never met any such people, but perhaps you'll be luckier?

But before you become wise and until you are happy with life and love, do this thing that the great, rich, incomparable, blessed Georgian language has no words for, and what, in the other languages I know, is termed 'make love.' When you don't want to make love any more, that's the time to speak about higher matters. Meanwhile, do it whenever and wherever you can. I don't think that either inside a dirty elevator or—very popular for some reason—by the sea (there's even a cocktail, do you remember, called 'orgasm on the beach'—if you haven't tried it, don't bother, it's indescribably horrible, it neither tastes good nor makes you drunk) are the best places for it. You will either hurt your knees, or bruise your back. But each to his own. If you like, you can do the business standing up in a hammock. The time and place is not any guarantee of success, all you have to consider is that if you have sex with someone, it should be a question of giving and taking, and not sex. If you just use someone, it is unlikely to bring you joy. When, in the Russian turn of phrase, 'the enemy of the people is fucked,' neither of the parties comes out smiling. At the end of the day, sex is not an execution.

Don't raise your fist to the colourful, joyful parrot with merciful Kama mounted on its back. He flew towards you to make your life a celebration. And if somebody does not like your ethics, they can avert their eyes from you. The main thing is that you should not be afraid of anything. If you are in a state of fear, neither sex nor, especially, love is of any good.

I wish you success.

With love,

Yours,

Ana Kordzaia-Samadashvili

P.S. Do you remember Caryl Chessman? I told you about him at the beginning. When he was tied up to the chair and he smelled the smell of gas, he turned to the reporters who had come to see his execution, and winked at them as if to say, 'I was joking. What's all the fuss about?'

BERIKAOBA

I can explain myself. I only made a mistake because the times were mixed up. There's no other way that I, the mother of Georgian mysteries and the shining light of Georgia, could make such blunder. What can you do? As the Russian proverb has it, even a marksman can sometimes miss.

Berikaoba, our Georgian masquerade theatre, takes place in the spring. I don't know why, but that's what I was taught. According to custom, when winter comes to an end, I think during the spring equinox, somebody, I don't know who—Enuki, Benuki or Bubuta—turns into the character of Berika, who is a man dressed as an animal. At the same time, the other characters become his accomplices. Berika makes your dreams come true. He burns all the useless things that have accumulated in the house or your head, defeats enemies, declares his love to you, sings and dances. When someone like him becomes very attached to you, eventually, if you aren't completely dead, you will probably begin to believe that a new life will start from now on, that you will be omnipotent, because you are strong, young, beautiful and generally very cool.

The whole gist is that one wonderful morning Berika again becomes Enuki, Benuki or Bubuta, and if you have any feelings on the subject, you should not get angry that he is not the same as he was yesterday. He is only like that while the show is going on, so that's why, when Berikaoba is over, you shouldn't have an existential crisis. I blamed myself for getting into such state when I was a drunkard. Thank God that only my four walls heard what was going on. Next year someone else will play Berika, or perhaps you will be Berika. It's better that way, isn't it?

One such Berika popped around to see me, only a bit out of season, in winter. It was one of those dreary Tbilisi winters, neither cold nor warm, and I felt the same way, lukewarm. Nothing exciting was happening, but nor did anything so horrible occur that I would have to kill myself or run to L. in some depressing place. I thought, all I need to do is get through this winter and see what will happen afterwards, and so I relaxed.

My Marco Polo arrived for the New Year from somewhere or other. I could not establish where from, as he recently lost his marbles, so that's why he's unable to narrate anything coherently. I wasn't at all happy to see him, because he's as unlucky as the number thirteen, and nothing good can happen when he appears with his shiny face. I have direct experience of this and am constantly aware of it. On the other hand, the poor soul himself isn't to blame. That's just the way he is; we can hardly kill him for it.

Obviously, I was full of joy at seeing a boyfriend after such a long journey. He gave me a sip of cognac from his flask, and to the delight of the people around us, and in order to give them something to gossip about, we kept shouting endearments at each other: 'my joy,' 'my life,' 'my sunshine.' Approximately one hour later, my joy and sunshine told me that he was back because he had missed the wife that he had abandoned some eight years previously. 'You know,' he said, 'she didn't have anyone after me.' 'What do you mean, no one?' My cognac went down the wrong way and I turned blue. 'It means she loves me,' he said. 'And now, I realise that I love her too.' I was naturally very pleased to hear that, but on the other hand, why did it get on my nerves? I knew he was an idiot, didn't I?

At the end of it all, we finished up in the house. We lay on mattresses on the floor in our trousers, boots, and coats. We lay there and the guy was dreaming. I'd give anything to dream an amazing dream like that.

'It's as if we are husband and wife, and we are lying all warm and cosy like this. We have to get up at six in the morning to go to the factory. We are working at the factory, which doesn't bother me. It's very cold outside, it's a proper winter. So we'll go to the factory and I'll be happy, because I will have lunch with you during the break, and we'll eat 'woe and venom,' and then, in the evening, we will go home together and will do everything together (I wonder what?), and then we will go to bed and, perhaps, have sex, but more likely not, because the following morning we will have to get up early again. What a great life! I will love you loads. How happy I am! Then in summer we'll take a holiday somewhere, probably to a spa, like Sairme, or somewhere like that, probably at the seaside, and after that we'll remember how we shagged for ages. Only later, you'll definitely get bored with me and you'll find a different job for sure, and when you go out, I'll know that you are seeing another man (how did you guess?), but I'll still love you a lot, and I won't say anything, and I will suffer (hallelujah!).'

I can't say anything about his suffering, but I suffered a lot! At one stage, when I was a younger and more optimistic woman, I loved that man and I didn't know that he was crazy, and, who knows, perhaps he loved me too, but only for a short while, and afterwards he didn't love me anymore, and I nearly went mad too. Now I'm lying next to him and I am only glad that his wishes aren't coming true, God save me from that.

Our relationship carried on in this way, until, during the third or fourth meeting, he completely lost the plot and drove me mad. Wife! Fuck your wife! He dragged her towards me at the table, the bastard, and was kissing her hands, my God! She was a nice girl, and it was that which probably made me finally flip. She was fair-haired, sophisticated, well dressed. She was weeping, but that suited her too. She wasn't a complete idiot and she didn't make up with him, but that was beside the point, because the whole story drove me mad anyway.

And then I remembered that several weeks earlier, God bless Marco, before Marco's arrival, I had seen a man and liked the look of him too, and thought that it would have been so nice to have something to cheer me up during winter. So when, one evening, 'the joy and angel' went out, I did something that was unexpected, even by my standards, I phoned him. And the man, whom I'll call Berika in this story, came to my home. I call him Berika because it doesn't matter what his name was, nor his surname, age, or social status. I assure you, he was Berika, and that's that. And so Keenoba, the fertility rites, and Berikaoba, the masquerade theatre, began during that dreary winter. To cut a long story short, I will be eternally grateful to that man and always remember the time fondly.

At one stage, I promised L. that I would save his letters so that when I became his biographer I could publish these epistles as an appendix. Together with everything else, I wrote to him about that equinox in the middle of January. I like to write everything down. In order for the reader to understand better the phenomenon of Berikaoba, apart from my story, told in this whinging manner, the reader should be aware of the existing background. This background is in this bundle of previously unmentioned letters from L.

Saturday, 18:34

Come on, Missus, the first shot has been fired so everything in your life will now be different. By the way, I could not find the Afghan military hat you wanted anywhere. It is a matter of political correctness.

L.

Thursday, 14:54

Where does Georgian moonshine, chacha, come from?
Life is endlessly fascinating. Keep me informed about how
things go.
God bless you that you write good things about yourself at least.

L.

That non-existent, but, at that time, flesh and blood man,
Berika, who had fallen from the sky, was too big for me. The
best thing was that he had big hands. When he arrived, he would
take off his rings and I was always surprised by his large fingers.
I could squeeze three of my own fingers into one ring. I told him
that wise men wore that particular stone in China. He laughed.
I liked him a lot.

And he was painted all over. That kind of painting is called
'tattooing' or something. I liked him an awful lot. I used to sit on
the edge of the bathtub, looking at him and trying to make out
what was painted on him, whether it was the sun, an eagle or
something else. At one stage, I very much wanted tattoos myself,
but I was afraid that I wouldn't be able to bear the pain and would
run away with a tattoo half-finished. He told me that it wasn't
painful at all.

He used to send me letters. He wasn't inquiring how I was but
wrote about other things. If he'd read something, he would send
a quotation, if not, he would simply write to me whatever came
into his mind. Well, how can I know so much Latin? I would ask
him what it meant. 'Like attracts like,' he said. Aha!

Each time he came, he brought something new. Secret flutes
murmured something quietly, this man was playing an unusual
instrument. I don't even know what this music is called. Sometimes he would tell foreign tales. I couldn't work out whether they

were sad or joyful. Sometimes they were about his travels and his adventures, and there were always beautiful women involved in the stories, who had a mesmerizing aura of eroticism. He was a good raconteur, very artistic. Perhaps the reason Berika was so convincing was due to these inherent artistic qualities. Once he brought some food and when he took it out of the shopping bag, the scene looked like an illustration from a fairy tale, with small, neat mushrooms, colourful pickles, and Georgian bread in the shape of fish, the kind of fish that swim in the warm waters of distant countries.

When we were alone, I was always happy when he was around, less so in the company of other people. Not only because it was an incredible love and my heart would stop when I saw him, but also because the others did not know that he was Berika. It seemed he had failed in his role too, and turned into an average guy, a seemingly successful Georgian man, exactly what he became after Berikaoba was over. Such types were like the colourful pebbles on a beach at the Black Sea, where they were always on the look-out for untanned women, that is, newly arrived and so far unattached.

L. was very happy. It seems he remembered his Berikaobas and he was delighted—and how delighted! Although he knew very well how such mysteries could end up, he, like me, hoped that this time someone would at least understand the essence of Berikaoba, and would not kill it off with their intolerance.

Thursday, 17:51

Write to me, Missus! What's new?
I saw Hans, and he said he is going to send you a parcel, but he told me in such manner that he probably hopes to send a huge one. I won't be able to take it. He put in some coffee, aspirin, a book by Yerofeev (in German; here, too, everyone's gone crazy) and I don't know what else.

Look how everything has turned out well.
Then we'll get you married off in Europe, to some rich guy, and
all of us will become prosperous. Before that, you work for a
while. But watch out that you don't bump into some shit. Let's
hope we won't get involved with any Young Communists.
With hope for a better life. Don't lose your optimism.
Best regards,

L.

Although I talk all the time, I could not tell Berika that he was
a good man. Somehow, I couldn't do it. Wow, how I was waiting
for Hans' coffee! I didn't have any money left, but I wanted Berika
to be happy about something else, for example Hans' coffee. But
it did not come in time, and that was for the best, because if he
had poured that coffee on my head I would have hit him with a
candlestick and then he would definitely have killed me.

But before it reached that point, he used to call out to me
from the car, and he was so aglow, that it was as if he saw, not me
in my puffa jacket with its cigarette burns, but Mata Hari dancing her striptease.

Saturday, 19:29

It's peaceful here.
Write and tell me who you are in love with. Is it the same per-
son as a month ago, or a new one?
Will you see a woman in Tbilisi or Yerevan?

L.

Later, according to the rules, it was time for Berika to go.
Berikaoba was over, as unexpectedly as it had begun.

One day, the guy was drinking tea, and he realised not just that the festivity was over but that I was not, after all, the golden-haired daughter of a king. He learned some even worse things. Ouch! That sometimes I like to drink too. I play backgammon well, and sometimes for money. Oh, how shameful it is to be spotted greeting such a woman in public so that everyone knows you are acquainted with her kind. It's especially so if you are a member of the elite and are on your way to watch some conceptual shit with a thoughtful expression on your face. And moreover, sometimes I'm broke. He could have asked me directly, and I would have told him that's the way I was. Bless!

To come to the point, the guy's eyes were open and he came out with such things! I remember what he said word for word, as well as every expression and gesture of that extraordinary man. I'm talking about the man I had known before that evening. One sentence was especially ironic to hear. 'What did you think—that I would support you?' That's when Keenoba, the fertility festival, Berikaoba, the masquerade, and Bairamoba, the feast, were all finally over. I phoned my favourite neighbour. He was an angel. He came, drank tea, and we played backgammon until morning. Thank goodness I wasn't alone in an empty house.

Probably you were disappointed, Berika, because I did not understand what you were dealing with, because you understand nothing about pagan feasts and you don't know that you could be proud of something. At least you were Berika once in your life.

Friday, 15:17

Such is life, Missus! There are pricks like that guy everywhere. Men like telling women what to do. So, don't worry. Anything else?
Go and see my house being decorated.
Is the situation still the same—that other guys, like Enuki,

Benuki and Bubuta, are happier than us?
My hello to that woman from Armenia. Give her some cash,
perhaps she may be useful.

L.

NINA

I was never a very close friend of Nina's. I can only take so much. She was an unbearable woman, God forgive me. Before Niko introduced her to me, I only knew a couple of things about her. But I was rather surprised: apparently she grew up in a good family, not in a jungle, she had a French governess, and she also knew several languages. Really, none of that was obvious. However, I immediately believed that she had lived all over the Soviet Union, because she was so good at adjusting to new places and she slept so soundly. Clearly she was a woman of the world. In addition, I knew she'd started out owning a restaurant, then moved into real estate, and then became a travel agent, and as soon as she got hold of some money, she would get a man too. After that, she would squander the money, and then it would all start again from the very beginning, searching for money and, accordingly, for a new man.

Niko introduced her to me in the ski resort of Gudauri. Nina was sitting in the foyer with a glass in her hand, talking incessantly. At that point, I didn't know that she was always in such a state, and I was surprised to hear what the matter with her was:

'Don't worry, I won't die so easily. You know, they told me my fortune. Forty years minimum. And in bed, a contented granny, with lots of grandchildren. You will have a rest when I'm pushing up the daisies. There's only one thing—where will all those grandchildren come from? It's a viral infection, isn't it? Shamanic old women, like fortune tellers, occasionally make mistakes too.'

But, as I found out later, she was a real coward. She was afraid of conflict, of enclosed spaces, and of being alone at night.

'The thing about night is not that I am afraid of wolves or thieves. I am afraid that something may frighten me. That's it and nothing else. When I was at Michael's, that genius first showed me around his house, with its cellars and secret doors. Yes, he really had a secret passage in the wall, because it's a sixteenth-century house. He did not complete the job of digging out the cellars. He didn't have enough money left to get the lower one cleared, and he was afraid of doing it himself. "What, do you think I was afraid of the dark, or because some buried Luther might come back from the dead? I was afraid that the house might have collapsed," he said. He's sick. I'm just saying that. Do you know how much I love him? So, he took me up to the garret, showed me the huge bed, it was a double bed, where I was supposed to sleep alone. I lived with my boyfriend during that whole year, yet the whole time, I was left on my own. My boyfriends were good people, it was just that I was alone and got a bit bored. Okay, I wasn't entirely alone, but I slept alone. Michael told me, very happily, that the house was completely insulated for sound and that outside voices would not bother me. Accordingly, if I screamed fit to burst, nobody would hear me. That's good, isn't it? Before I went to bed, I thoroughly checked out the loft so that I wouldn't confuse the wardrobe for the ghost of somebody's lost soul. There was a mirror in the corner too. Imagine if that started gleaming at night? I threw myself onto the bed, I read *The History of Ancient Rome*, and then turned off the light. A bell rang once every fifteen minutes, as there was a church in that street, and it nearly drove me mad. In this kind of place, no one gives a shit about the bell ringing, or about anything else. The town is so quiet, it's a nightmare. I can't stand such peaceful towns. The very next day I ran away. I told Michael that I had a romantic rendezvous. God forgive me for lying. Otherwise, I'm not fearful at all. What do I have to be afraid of? What, will I die, or what?'

Niko got involved. 'No, you won't die, they'll kill you.' He wasn't looking at Nina, and in fact she wasn't exactly much to look at.

'No, they won't kill me, that's nonsense. I should have died many times before, and I didn't. I didn't even get an upset stomach. I told you, didn't I?'

***

Just like many other pseudo-intellectuals, Nina had read thousands of incomprehensible books, such as meditation bibles by Osho and various kinds of feminist rubbish. That's why, apart from the stuff of everyday life, her head was full of silly ideas. I used to meet her, without Niko, at Soso's club. She came up with an explanation when yet another of her three-week-long love affairs of her not very long life came to an end. Such an explanation could only have occurred to her, because Nina was a cretin:

'You know there's nothing wrong with me, and I was in good shape then. I had more money than anyone in my family has ever had. I also liked the business I was in, I had a house and I also thought I looked beautiful, with a summer suntan, I don't know, it didn't bother me to be without a man either, I don't know. So, because I'm an idiot, when I was lying on the beach, I recalled, you know how it is, my girl, I remembered something very cool. That's how it goes, when the sun sets, you have to make a wish, a wish with your whole heart, and it will come true. I'm telling you so that you know that you have to ask for it properly, or the same will happen to you as happened to me. I miscalculated and asked God to give me love for at least a week, or two weeks, and after that I would put up with anything, I said. So, he gave it to me, for a week or two, and then when it was over, I asked him—not the man, but God—why was he so mean? Why was it just for one or two weeks? He said that he gave me what I asked for. Can you imagine that?'

It's obvious that people must often cry in this club. Nina was crying openly but nobody could care less. Through the open window, there was a child who was grimacing at her mother. There were lots of plants in lots of pots. It was hot. Nina wiped her nose with a green handkerchief.

I will never cry in public. A weeping woman looks like a monkey. And Nina, with her skull shaved, skinny, once tanned but now with the skin peeling on her arms, at that time still thought she could wear a short dress. Only later did she begin to remember her blue veins. Later she told me, 'When I see my reflection in a shop window, I always want somebody to shout, "Pele! Goal, goal!"' Before she met that man, she couldn't have cared less whether she had beautiful knees or not. 'For goodness sake, Nina, as if you have nothing better to think about!' she thought to herself.

'Come on, as if you have nothing else to do apart from thinking about your legs! What does it matter? He didn't tell me to piss off because of my legs. That singer, Zempira, is good, isn't she? She's a nice girl. You know that Krishna demands everything from his loyal followers. It seems that Krishna loves me a lot, and he was jealous. You know, the dancing god, Krishna, the colour of thunder clouds, the one who attracts everybody and everything. Shit! Are they ever going to bring our beer or do I need to call the police?

'You know what I'll tell you? Here we are, he's bringing the drinks. So, when you bump into a man who is endlessly talented, senselessly educated, and difficult, and, at the same time, a fucker, you have to run away instantly, for example to somewhere like Trebizond. If you are a fool and don't run away, you should at least acknowledge that everything is a total lie. I just did not understand the logic. Shit, I was with him anyway and I was shagging him, so what else could I do? I was mad about him, and getting what the hell I wanted. I didn't need his "wow" and "hey" declarations of love, thank you very much.' She turned, beaming, to the waiter, 'Don't worry, please, I have an allergy and that's why

I look like I'm covered in mosquito bites. Your beers look great!'

This foolish, and totally irritating, love story began foolishly too. Niko took Nina to some foreign diplomatic representative's office, and a week later helped her to sell three apartments in the central Vake district of Tbilisi. The girl got some money. With that money she bought a pair of sandals, three sizes too big. Like the fairy tale character, Little Mook, she intended to grow into the slippers. She also bought a patterned Indian scarf, which she either wrapped around her waist, or neck, or she used it as a towel, and sometimes as a tablecloth. And with the rest of the money, she was going to go to Olympus to get a tan, to bathe in the blue sea, and to smoke dope on the pink rocks. She was just telling us all about her glorious plans in the café when she met a man there.

Why she liked him, I can't tell you. Nina's way of evaluating men clearly has nothing to do with what happened in this instance. But I must say one thing—they resembled each other, both in appearance and, as it seemed to me then, in other ways too. Perhaps it was because they both travelled a lot, they are both off their heads with Eastern mysticism, or perhaps, a mixture of the two. Who knows—and this also sounds a bit naff—maybe they both felt terribly lonely, and both thought, here we are, our dreams have come true! I can't speak for the man, but Nina was besotted. Nina is an idiot.

The fact is, that evening, while he was talking to Nina, a girl he knew approached him. She had large tits and surgically-enhanced lips, and was much younger and sexier than Nina. The man told the girl that he and Nina were going to Turkey. The girl sulked. The following day, in the same café, the man told Nina that he couldn't go to Turkey after all because Sopho was still young, while Nina was a brave woman who would be okay without him. Nina told him that there was no question that she would be okay. That evening she went to a bar on Perovskaya Street and got drunk on vodka, and the following day, as usual, she spent alone. She did not suffer too much, it seems that she was used to such stuff happening. If it was me, for example, I would have committed suicide.

Clearly, if she had had any brains at all, she wouldn't have come to the café under any circumstances, but whoever heard of Nina having a brain? She thought she looked great after her time at the seaside, and she sat at the same table, hoping to see the same man.

The atmosphere became full of Southern passion. Nino went mad. She had to get up at eight in the morning to get to the swimming pool early enough so she wouldn't be late for work. Of course, she needed to keep up her suntan! Under any other circumstances, nobody could force Nina to enter the water. She was a really hard worker and she wanted money. To put it in a nutshell, she went crazy. Then, in the same crazy manner, she ran to that man. They rolled around on the sofa, dreaming of how they would travel across half the world, how they would love each other, and how their souls would be blessed.

The first blunder occurred when she said 'I' instead of 'we.' 'I will go.'

'I thought I could not give a shit. But I did give a shit. Then he started haranguing me in Russian, asking the usual questions blokes ask: "When were you last with a man? Do you shave your legs?" Don't you know I don't shave, you shit? I cut it. Moron! And yet more classic questions: "Did you come?" Yes, I had a fantastic orgasm, if that's what you want to hear, yes, classic: "Have you finished?" Maddening.'

To cut it short, she didn't go to Olympus. She didn't have so much money left, but they went to Batumi together. They stayed there for a week, hanging around. He went swimming. Nina couldn't swim, and when they came back, the man told her, 'Bye bye, sister, you take care of yourself and I'll take care of myself.' I'm not surprised that it ended like that, how could that poor man bear Nina? Were his nerves so strong? To be with Nina constantly for a week, moreover to be with Nina in love, how could anyone bear it?

So what did I say to her?

Do you know that rap song? She got up and performed it skilfully. People at the table in the corner table looked up and stared at Nina foolishly.

What does it mean?

Everything has one ending, only a sausage has two. That's how it is, my treasure, that's how it is my treasure!

That night, I went with her to a discotheque full of gays, and the next day, Nina went to the seaside again and when she returned, she had neither a man, nor a business, nor worries about either of them. At least, that's what she said. It's only now that I've bumped into her again, in winter. Did I really have time for Nina then?

As I informed you, the season was foul, it was winter and it was a dull evening too. I was going up the hill and I met Nina near the shop where I always avoid stopping, because I owe them money.

She looked terrible. The mauve coat she was wearing suited her as much as white aprons suit bears in the circus. It was obvious that she was drinking again: her eyes were sunken and her nose was peeling.

She went into the shop and paid off my debts, and purchased her typical selection of goods. She was a vegetarian, but instead of beer she bought vodka, a lot of it, because, she said, it was cold. When we got to my house, I lit the gas cooker and I gave Nina some of my clothes. One of her socks was shamefully torn, and she complained that it was rubbing her between her toes. Then I asked why she didn't buy new ones, she had money. She replied, 'Come on!'

Okay. We filled our glasses. Nina sat with her leg tucked under her. Once, I was surprised how she was able to do that, then I found out that, at some stage, she had been a ballerina, then she became obsessed with hatha yoga and her straight back was a left-over from those days: 'Aging begins from here.' She used to stroke her neck, carefully, because she had a mole there and she was afraid of melanoma. She still sat with a straight back, but she had aged a lot.

She straightened her elbow, picked up the glass and started proposing a toast:

'Be happy, my beauty. I wish you everything that I wish for myself when I am in a good mood. First, good health. Imagine if you had toothache, would you be able to do anything? A long life, travel, a gorgeous man—healthy, talented, handsome, kind, wealthy, generous. Why would you want a coward and a miser? Also, he should be in love with you, and you should be mad about him, but he should be more mad. To cut it short, be cool! I love you very much and in my future life I will be born as a man, and at first, you won't love me, but I will fight for you and marry you, and you will be the happiest woman alive.'

Apparently, Nina had been a happy child. Apparently, everybody loved her: her extremely erudite mother, her amazing father, grandfather, and a degenerate brother who had 'emigrated to Finland.' They say her grandmother loved her too, only Nina didn't remember her, as she was three when she died. Her grandmother had been run over by a car and the presents she'd bought for Nina fell out of her bag. That woman was called Nina too. They told Nina stories about how her granny was beautiful, but added that Nina didn't look like her.

'I don't look like her on the outside, but I probably resemble her in some ways. It seems that my granny used to be a very strong-minded lady, and in general all the women on my mother's side were not quite all there. I shouldn't say "were." It's still the case.'

'What do you mean by that? Why are you picking up on that?'

'Come on, you know full well that I'm not all together, either. And now my memory is giving out. I've got a good command of language, but what else can I say? Well, first it was all about "that beauty Margarita." If you knew the story, you would understand what the matter is with me.'

Nina never asked whether you wanted to know her stories.

'To get to the point, that Margo is buried there, in the village where I was sent every summer of my childhood, the village that I hate. Now, if you wanted to, we could go there. In fact, it's a cool place.' She stretched out a bony arm. 'There's a spring there as wide as my wrist, and there's a pine forest there too, a simple forest, with mushrooms, I don't know. You could go nuts there from boredom. All you can hear is, "Hey, hey," followed by "Cheep, cheep," as Aunty Patso sprinkles corn for the chicks. She's ground the corn, so that it won't get stuck in their throats, nothing must get stuck in the chicks' throats. Shit, I love hens so much. Only when they are alive. Roosters even more. Oh, come on! Let's go for a day or two! It isn't hard to get there. It's a beautiful house, half an hour from the station, okay, one hour. I really hate it, but if you came . . . Let's go. There are old magazines. Have you read the story called "I'm the King"? Let's go , let's go . . .'

She drank. Niko said that they had been planning to go to that village for one hundred years, ever since they met each other.

'So, Margarita was a beautiful woman and was mad about herself. She was a lady-in-waiting, or maid-of-honour, or something like that in the governor's house. Perhaps that's why I have pretensions to the minor aristocracy. Only she didn't marry. Perhaps it was because she was crazy, or wasn't quite all there, or had taken a vow of celibacy. I don't know what it was all about. I'm convinced Granny Knaro makes this moonshine by boiling up the old padded waistcoat they gave her to wear in the camps! Do you think it will make me go blind? So, when Margarita was thirty she looked in the mirror and saw a wrinkle. Can you imagine? I've had wrinkles since I was twenty. She went to the gates of the village cemetery. Before that she had ordered a tombstone made of Venetian marble, nothing else would suit her. The stone, with its angels and roses, which now lays on her heart, she kept under her bed and lived like that for one hundred years. I know from the family that the stone is Venetian, otherwise how could I know about it? They were always going on about how it was Venetian, and that Margarita was very beautiful, and that these petty gentry were pains in the arse. Every time I go there they tell me that story. I don't remember how long exactly, but she lived a long life. I don't understand how it is that she's my granny, but she lies in my mother's family burial plot. Guess how she was off her head? Guess what this village is like now; and can you imagine what it was like then?'

'I don't know.'

'What don't you know? Is this normal? The main thing is that we should be well.' She poured, but didn't drink. 'Say something.'

'You say something.'

I had nothing to say.

'Okay. To a bright future. How lovely to be a thirty-five-year-old girl with all your potential. What future have I got? It all looks like shit, just black soil falling on my coffin.'

She drank. Then she went out to the loo and I could hear her singing a Russian folk song from there.

'*My sweetheart is probably coming* . . . What did you say?'

'Nothing.'

'Yes, where's Niko?'

'He said he will be here soon.'

'What?'

'He'll be here soon.'

'Aha.'

Nina and Niko became friends at some point long ago. Nina

didn't love anyone in the world more than she loved Niko. I think
she didn't love anyone at all, and when she got very drunk, she
said that, if God loved her, she and Niko would have loved each
other. He would have been happy and she would have been happy. But that's not true because Nina would not have been happy.
She is one of those who is only happy if she's unhappy, and Niko
likes young women. All Nina's men were a bit jealous of Niko,
but mistakenly, because Nina would rather have joined a convent than have anything to do with Niko. She used to quote the
Russian saying, 'Life is sweet with its memories.' She was logical
about Niko but not about other things.

Any mention of Niko usually led to a long tirade. Nina knew
very well that I did not want to listen to this anymore, that's
why she tried to excuse herself by telling silly stories. I'm very
surprised that the alcohol she's poured into herself for all these
years hasn't deprived her of the ability to remember things, or the
ability to speak.

'Then, when Atmananda and I walked in the street for the
whole night, in Leningrad—wow, the mosquitoes were huge,
you know. Atmananda said that, when she was in the madhouse
there, the doctor told her that a tendency to speak in monologues
is the first sign of schizophrenia. That's probably what I've got,
haven't I?' She didn't wait for an answer and poured some more.
At first she poured a little bit at a time, but later she added more.
'Drink. Then, we'll run to the loo. Poor Atmananda, she died
from, what do you call it, botulism? Let's turn to Niko! He's proof
of the existence of Georgian men, my Nikoloz. When I get rich,
I don't know what I will do for him. Anything! I will give him an
allowance, a good one, and I will tell him that he's been awarded a
research grant. But my imagination is limited, isn't it? *Gaumarjos!*
Cheers! Good health! Niko is the best. Let him be very happy,
successful, let him have money, a great love. In short, let him have
whatever he wishes. *Gaumarjos!*'

We drank. She reached for a mandarin, but the thing is that she does not like that particular fruit. So she must have been drunk.

'Nina, shall we go to bed? I have to leave tomorrow.'

'Yeah, go to bed. I'll have a shower, okay? And I'll come to bed after that. I'll switch off the boiler and the light too. Don't worry.'

In the morning I discovered that she'd left and that she'd never come to bed. She probably preferred to have a nice sleep at home. She had washed up the dishes and she had picked the dry leaves off the potted plants. I phoned her, but she didn't answer. Then her mother told me that she had gone to Puna to study. She had rented out her apartment and left, but would return in a couple of months. But if you remember, she kept on saying, 'Osho is no longer there, so what would I want in Puna?' It seems she felt cold, so she decided to spend the winter there and will come back.

***

She had noticed that slope leading down to the river, near the bridge, several years ago, when she was learning to drive a car. She used to wait for the instructor's blue car at the corner of the bridge, three times a week, at nine o'clock. She wanted to learn to drive so she could travel around Turkey.

Her legs were frozen cold. She had warm boots, but she didn't wear them. She said the top of the boots were too wide so she couldn't easily press the brake pedal. Those high-heeled shoes didn't go well with her trousers. Well, nobody knows who she was trying to impress. The instructor? I don't think so. To cut it short, she used to stand there and freeze, looking at the scenery. That's when she discovered that slope.

She filled a rucksack with rocks and crystals from the mountains, which she had taken from home. She adjusted it carefully and set off.

'Can you imagine how much river water I've drunk? I've sipped from the Danube and also from the Argun in Mongolia. Who knows how many Ninas were in the water? How did I survive such poison?'

Perhaps, that's what she was thinking. I don't know exactly.

Nina was stupid. She thought that if she had a rucksack full of stones, she wouldn't float to the surface, and everyone would think that she had gone to Puna.

BON VOYAGE

Maia has arrived. Nothing's changed. She was late again and to get to the finishing line, that's to say, my place, she ran all of ten meters. She's a silly woman.

She's become very attractive. She's lost weight and bought some new things. We had seven *laris* between us, with which we bought beer and chips. We sat there for a long time. Russian songs were bellowing out in the restaurant and various people were trying to call me, but I wasn't answering. Maia's shoes felt tight and she put her feet up. That's how things were then, in winter.

We drank all winter long and we ran up debts. We ate potatoes. I kept a sack of them in the cellar. When it was finished, we didn't eat anything more, we just drank. I cried every night, sometimes she did too, sometimes just me, sometimes both of us together. We would get drunk, then we did foolish things, and then we phoned each other, we got together, drank and cried. In the mornings we would rub some ice on our faces and make an attempt to earn money. That winter, absolutely everybody used us and let us down. They would not return money they owed me and all of Maia's business affairs failed. Then she had a dream that we were swimming together somewhere, in water full of cigarette butts, gobs of spit, and dirt, and that we clung to each other. Then I cursed, using foul language about the mother of my beloved man and calling my God deaf. Maia sold the house. I found a job, and she went away.

Now we're together again. I'm telling her that I can no longer wear short dresses because they don't suit me anymore. Maia tells me that we will go to the seaside, we'll get suntanned, and I will have beautiful legs again. I tell her that if someone doesn't like the look of me, they can start looking the other way.

Since Maia left, I haven't spoken to anyone. She has been silent too, up until today, because she didn't speak the language of this country. We decided that we would live differently from now on, that we wouldn't moan any more and we wouldn't drink. We would go to the bathhouse, exercise, and wouldn't think any more about the fact that Maia's men either die or end up in the madhouse. As for my men, it's very simple: they don't love me.

Why should they—can you tell me?

Because we are golden girls. Okay, we have stretch marks, cellulite, difficult personalities and we are horrible drunks, but so what? But then, what about those others, the ones who have excessive body hair, and big and unjustified ambitions but no money—they don't have a future because there's no chance of them finding a promising man under forty. What do you think of that?

In the morning I told Maia that I had seen somebody in my dream. He was called Ariel.

'How do you know? Was he a kind angel or one of those coming for your soul?'

'He was kind, of course!'

It's August now. In two months, winter will begin. In January, Dato will come for a month, and I'll be happy for a while. Then spring will come, Maia will go to seek her fortune and I will find a new job. All will be well. Won't it?

MY FRIEND, MARISHA

If you ask me, she's a rather beautiful woman. She is short but very neat, and she has breasts enough for two women. She is blonde-haired and it's dyed. As far as I can remember, her natural colour was chestnut. Her blonde hair hung down to her bottom, and her bottom, wow, what can I say? Eventually, she cut that wonderful hair. Ultimately, it was just long and useless. She did it with a pair of crooked scissors, but that happened towards the end. But before that, Marisha, with her Georgian name but very Slavonic appearance, lived in the sunny city of Tbilisi, where she weaved tapestries in the Gobelin style and considered herself very lucky.

The major problem with Marisha was her rather strange religiosity. I don't know anyone else who would call on Saint Nicholas whilst boiling lentils, imploring him in Russian, 'Do your best, dearest one.' While saying confession, she wept, not because she was repenting, but with love. I'm not joking. I should also inform you that Marisha had such a personal relationship with God and His entourage that it never occurred to her to observe periods of fasting or similar obligations. She managed her relationship with them perfectly well without such things. I was very surprised when many years later, she wrote, also in Russian, 'I know that God exists and that I have some kind of relationship with Him, but what kind of relationship, I don't know and I don't want to know.' Marisha's progress through life was strange, but let's talk about that later.

Inevitably, being pretty and lively, and obviously young, Marisha was immediately spotted by various Venerable Fathers who made sure it was her destiny to get married. Evil tongues whispered about how one of them had married a Russian woman. What do you expect, even though the Slavonic half of Marisha's make-up wasn't of Russian origin? The man had a wonderful voice. He could make his eyes flash and he treated his wife very strictly. The problem was that, when it came to 'doing the business,' he was completely useless. He was a total virgin and, to put it crudely, he couldn't get his dick up. Marisha would probably have ended her life as a virgin if it hadn't been for the other neighbour, Alochka, a former hippy, half-mad as a result of poor-quality drugs. She talked some sense into Marisha and then she went to church to face the priest. She cursed Father Zpsome, or perhaps he was called Soprom, I don't remember exactly, there's been a lot of water under the bridge since then. She called the priest impotent, and told him to 'fuck off' twice. With the blessing of Marisha's mother, she dispatched Marisha to the Baltic to stay with her old friend and fellow-warrior, Marietta, in order that Marisha would come to her senses and understand something of real life.

As you know, there were big upheavals in the Baltic countries at the beginning of the '90s, especially, and you probably don't know this, with Marietta in the background. During these momentous events, some *Stolichni*, that's to say guy from the capital, appeared with a great fanfare in Marisha's life. He was broad-shouldered and barrel-chested. Together with many other merits, this man had Latvian citizenship, a three-bedroom flat, and not entirely groundless claims to being a genius. Such were his amazing talents, Marisha's ability to weave Caucasian Gobelin-style tapestries is barely worth mentioning, but everything else, such as her plump breasts and delightful eyes, completely satisfied Stolichni. A great love, sex, and chaos ensued. What exactly our hero was doing in this respect is unknown and Marisha can't explain either. The fact is that, three months later, I bumped into Marisha in Moscow, in a communal flat. She wore huge glasses, her pinned-up hair was falling down, her dress was flapping around her ankles, and she'd completely lost the ability to communicate. She asked, 'Would you like some soup made of crusts of bread?' The poor woman was fasting.

This communal flat was a weird place. Marisha led her entire existence in one room. She ate, slept, prayed and howled there. Another room was occupied by an alcoholic called Slavik and his Armenian wife, Karina, from Tbilisi. Slavik cleaned his finger nails with a kitchen knife. Karina would tell me in Georgian, with her eyes sparkling, how she would murder Slavik as soon as she got her Moscow registration documents. Slavik's own comment on the situation never varied, 'Fuck the lot of you!' I never heard him say any other words, and probably the same applied to Karina. In the third room, they told me, lived a man, whose name remains unknown, even today. The women only saw him twice and called him kozlik, 'goat' in Russian, so I won't waste any more time telling you about him.

As I have said before, religion played an important role in Marisha's life. And, as a direct result of fasting and paying visits to the church, Marisha met a baptised Jew, about a hundred years older than her, and a poet. Karina referred to him in Russian as 'an intelligent all-rounder.' I never got so much as a glimpse of him, glory be to God! Marisha married him. We must give Marisha due credit: before she married this Jewish troubadour, she had plenty of sex with him, in order to avoid the mistakes she'd made with her previous marriages. Danger, as you know, is the colour of water, so you can't always see it. Not even Alochka saw the danger coming, even though she was a thousand times more experienced in such troublesome matters.

One sunny morning, the poet pulled out a knife and said to Marisha, 'I know your treachery, you whore!' and then proceeded to slice her a couple of times. Later that evening, in the hospital, it transpired that the man had spent a long time in KGB solitary confinement. He'd taken thousands of strange medications and, given the genetic disorders in his background, he had been diagnosed as a paranoid schizophrenic. Well, there you go. The man ended up in a clinic, and Marisha returned to the Baltics.

Stolichni, by that time, had completely changed his sexual orientation, therefore Ralph gave her his flat, because he was going to Saudi Arabia. When he returned, a huge telephone bill awaited him, the fridge was full of cigarette ends, and a huge sign in the doorway spelled AAA. Marisha was nowhere to be seen.

Apparently, her mother, frightened forever by events in Georgia, ran away to Moscow and rented a flat in Yasenevo, an area which was, in Alochka's words, the very arsehole of the city. Marisha had returned to her mother again. Several years later, in that ghastly flat, in the kitchen, she told me the story about her times in the Baltics. Apparently, mad with hunger and loneliness, she, together with another beauty from Vologda, found an excellent so-called 'office job' at the newspaper.

After an interview and an external examination, they were promised a hundred dollars as prostitutes, and, what a stroke of luck, on the very first occasion, she was introduced to a young, romantic, and wealthy man, who became mad about Marisha. Marisha, too, fell in love with that stag. Two weeks later, the man disappeared, and, instead of him, two bulls knocked on her door. No one knows what the hell they were looking for, but the fact is that they turned the house upside down, and it was Marisha who had to tidy it up afterwards. To bring the show to a striking finale, they threw her into their car, drove her to the cemetery and beat her up so badly that the beatings she had from Stolichni and the Jewish poet were like lullabies in comparison.

When I asked her what she did, I knew it was a stupid question, but I thought maybe she did her tapestry, I don't know. 'Can't you see?' Marisha replied, 'I'm cutting hashish.' What could I say? I could see that for myself. To be brief, life was very hard.

'Those goats!' howled Marisha in Russian, 'they couldn't even make babies for me. Every time I sat on one of them, I asked the Virgin Mary to make a baby for me, but, no, it didn't work. Fuck!'

It appeared the one she was lamenting now (as they say, 'the coffin is never empty') was a successful photographer, a former Tbilisi guy with a typical Georgian understanding of how to be a mate. He told Marishkina who those abusers were, and how dare they insult him by their deeds, and that he would blow up their mothers. For good measure, he added, he would fuck his own mother too, for her sake. First he said he would go to the Caucasus, to the war, where he would make money, and he would also take photographs to leave as his legacy. Then he would marry her, and give her children, and, for good measure, he would fuck his own mother again too, for her sake. Meanwhile, Marishka-was looking for work. (She failed to get a job as a waitress because they said she was too old and too short.) While the guy was standing in front of the mirror, combing his hair, speaking, blah-blah-blah, and being a total fuckwit, she was talking about her desire for a white dress, with layers of net, hand-embroidered and so on. Stupid woman! But, instead of fucking his own mother, that good man fucked over Marisha. He got hold of some money and after that no one ever saw him again.

Well, what else can I say? I haven't even had a glimpse of Marisha for four years and now, at the beginning of autumn, I received a letter, can you imagine?

She'd written in Russian: Where are you? I'm in Paris. Listen to an old woman as she tells you that cohabitation with people of the opposite sex is purely a societal pressure of our times. Do you think I am going to be pushing a pram in front of the house? Don't even think of it, madam! God be with us, and fuck them. Marisha.

A WONDERFUL EVENING

*After so many winters, it no longer matters who or what is standing
at the corner of the window with a blind.*

—Joseph Brodsky

Once, there was a man—let's not make a secret of it, I was very
keen on him—who asked me a surprising question: 'You do like
women, don't you?'

Actually, no, I don't like them. Nor do I like men, children,
the elderly, or people in general. Nor am I crazy about animals
and plants either. My heart is full of hatred. I didn't say so to that
man. As a good woman I couldn't possibly say such things. But I
was foolish. Why was I so coy? If I had spoken up, he would have
left me, and we would not have ended up hating each other. I'm
an idiot.

Several years ago a man, a different one, decided to create a
dream-come-true for a child of the Soviet era. Do you remember
the scene in *Roman Holiday* when the princess eats ice cream?
Didn't it make you want the same thing? He bought me a big
ice cream, with colourful balls of raspberry, chocolate, and mint
flavours. It is an entirely sickening story, but because I lived at
this man's expense, I shamelessly exploited his generosity. He still
loved me and thought of me as a human being. I ate all this horror and kept saying, 'yum, yum,' and at the railway station of some
godforsaken 'burg' I developed a sudden upset stomach.

I wish I could have one now. A sudden upset stomach is a glorious thing. You go mad with pain and sweat profusely. And of
course, the best place to have one is in some rural backwater where
your loose, black, unbrushed hair stands out a mile, and where

the only people dressed like you are washed-up drug addicts. The main thing is that, in this country, they can't stand foreigners, especially sick and poor ones. As the proud bearer of all these privileges, I lay on the platform and looked up at the unfamiliar sky. Oh well, death has arrived, and where am I but in some rotten hole, where a policeman with a beer belly will look down at me with contempt? I can imagine the expression on his face.

I am sitting in the kitchen, looking at the man who, at one stage, loved me, but who now thinks I am a drunk, moody, and unsuccessful lesbian, and he feels sick. And I hate him, oh yes, I hate this man, my God. And I remember that station, the smell of the deodorant, bought at considerable expense, and of the hand that covered my face, and how I was dying but did not die, and I won't die now either. You, young man, won't you ever go away?

I can't understand why I let this man get so close to me. I cannot understand, either, when it was we started hating each other. I have never been involved in such a situation before and at the moment I've got no idea how I should behave, that's why I'm staring at the wall and not speaking, a rare occurrence in my life. I'm thinking about that hot summer. The train has pulled in and it will leave in three minutes, but I can't get up from the filthy platform and no one even looks my way. The well-organised burghers of the town are getting on the train and I have to get on too or else I will be left here as a monument. Come on, you have to get on it, somehow, on all fours, crawling, because there won't be another train until tomorrow, and you have no money for another ticket, and you won't be able to hitch a lift from a car anywhere either, because you won't be able to crawl to the motorway. I try to remember the twelve prayers of Saint Ivlita and Saint Ieli. I manage to get onto all fours, then more or less up onto my two feet, and climb into the carriage, pressing my bag to my chest. I fall into a deep sleep until the conductor stands over me and shouts in his coarse voice something that sounds like 'Deutschland überalles.'

This one shouted at me too. Excuse me? His expression suggests that he thinks I am deaf too, poor me. If he hates me so much, I wonder why he has dragged himself here. I asked him why he was so sad, but I should have asked him instead why he was so mad. Well, I'm an idiot. His answer was 'What did you expect?' It was a peculiar conversation.

I've had some even better conversations. 'Don't make any unnecessary movements or I will hit you,' he said. Aha! And at that time, I was on alien territory, in the flat of the golden boy himself, but I had some money so I hailed a taxi and went home. When I got home, I turned the radio on loudly so that the neighbours couldn't hear my sobbing, and so they wouldn't tell my mother that she had a crazy daughter. They were playing a Russian song that went, 'It serves you right!' Neither the vocals nor the melody were any good, but the lyrics were brilliant. I enjoyed it a lot, but, as you see, I survived, and therefore I can bear his angry silence too. I wonder what's wrong with this man?

The main thing is not to be sorry for myself. Don't show that you are upset and that you are going crazy from loneliness, and you wish there would be gas explosions. There's silence again. The man has a radio on his lap, it's dusty, and I can see from his eyes that he thinks I am a dirty pig too. He told me a story about that woman, that woman who is not a pig like I am but a turtle dove. Oh well. I couldn't give a shit about that woman, or anyone, I just want to know what's wrong with this man. Why is he trying so hard to treat me like a doormat, and why don't I tell him to go away from my house? Why don't I tell this pleb and scum to go away?

In good weather, you can see the magical mountain ridge, Ialno, and the white rock faces. At one stage, I thought I would show this man our mountain hut and tell him how Alika loved the wolf, Mikaela, and how Vache and I went hunting for water in the dry gorge. For some reason I thought that.

This night will pass and this man will eventually go away. The main thing is to remember that hatred is a powerful thing and I will survive that too.

AUTUMN AND THAT LOVELY MAN

The day passes but problems remain.
> —Armenian proverb

The previous night I had to leave late. The metro was closed, then I confused a river with a canal and ended up in the Jewish quarter, where I had no business to be, then the strap of my rucksack broke and my shoulder hurt, and I got fed up and wet, and all in all, I am just a little girl, a bit more than thirty years old, and I can only take so much. When the telephone woke me up in the morning, I rushed out to the hallway in a fury—heaven knows why: no one would ever be phoning me in that house, but it was as if I was intending to tear the telephone off the wall and throw it away. Well, that's how it all began.

Nikoliko was standing in the corridor stark naked, or Nicole or Nick, or Nikipore. I will explain this now. Nicole is a feminist, at least she thinks she is. But, if you ask my opinion, she is a bit feeble-minded, preferring Nick to Nicole because she obviously thinks that Nick sounds more androgynous and cool. I personally, being a Georgian, prefer the sweet diminutive, Nikoliko, but if she makes me angry, and she often does, I call her Nikipore, my block-headed monkey.

It was the end of November, but we didn't switch the heating on as a matter of principle. Why? Nobody knows. That's why it was so cold, and especially cold in the hallway.

Nikoliko was talking to her juggler girlfriend on the phone. I could hear the girlfriend down the line, recounting at top speed a nightmare she'd had the previous night; I understood everything was very bad. I thought it would be better if I passed poor Nick her jacket, but then I realised that she could have reached it herself. I dragged myself to bed in order to carry on sleeping.

It goes without saying I was woken up again. This time it was Nikipore arguing. Apparently her mobile phone service had been disconnected. Aha. Okay. She was sitting in the kitchen with a man. He was dressed very smartly, fit to be buried, in a shirt which had been ironed by my own golden hands, and Nick was stark naked.

Do you know what the difference is between nude and naked? Nude is good, naked is shameful. Naked people wander around Tbilisi's 'Rainbow Bathhouse,' or the asylum, or they drink cold coffee together in a cold kitchen with two fully dressed people. The naked one is cold and blue, she's warming the soles of her feet by rubbing them against her calves, and her presence is totally unerotic.

When the poor man finished sipping his coffee—there was nothing else for him to enjoy there—and went off to take photographs of the bridges (goodness, what a glorious occupation, especially on an empty stomach and in the melting piles of snow), I told Nikoliko that the erotic show was over and she had to put on her clothes, otherwise I would be the one getting cystitis. Nikoliko proudly told me that the erotic had nothing to do with anything, and that she could not care less what feelings her body awoke in some dirty-minded man, and, she continued, her voice rising to a crescendo, anyone who didn't like it could get out of her house, because it was she who paid the rent, and that all men were degenerates, and it was obviously the case that some women were too. She pointed at me, her finger shaking from cold and anger, and said I clearly didn't understand anything about gender politics, and Nick's soul and vocation. She then stubbed her bare toe on a chair, which hurt her and she calmed down. Then Nikoliko cried a bit, went to her room, and returned dressed. She even put on some underwear in my honour, and told me that she did not like herself, in fact, she hated herself (another crescendo), and some idiot psychologist had recommended that she should walk around naked, but she was cold! And she hated herself. And to top it all, her mobile phone had been disconnected.

I left the house in good time and watched healthy guys jogging on the embankment. I smoked half a box of cigarettes, got hungry, swallowed some pita bread, and with both my stomach and mood in a heavy state, I went to earn my living. I work at the Literature Society in order to demonstrate my big intellect, ancient roots, and genuine talent.

In that good country, it seems to be permanently dark. Then it got even darker, it was night. I was late for my meeting with Anri. On my way there, I bought pita bread again, because I was hungry, but it's hard to walk quickly whilst chewing. Anri is an angel. He treats me to drinks, but not food every evening. He spends a lot on me, and isn't mean at all, he just probably thinks that I never eat. At our first meeting, I drank on an empty stomach, and I got so drunk that I did a belly dance in a Kurdish restaurant, and after that, a bit of Cossack dancing on the banks of the river. Anri is usually delighted when I do such things, but I don't like it at all.

Anri likes to see me home, on foot. I'm not keen on that. But that's not a problem, in twenty minutes we were home. We were met at the doorway by Nikoliko's juggler girlfriend and Margo; they were ringing the doorbell hysterically. Nick was not opening the door. They were in a state and informed me that they had arranged to come around half an hour before, and here we are, but she wasn't opening the door. 'She's killed herself,' the juggler concluded.

I opened the door and Anri, who was in any case a good man, came up too. He didn't want me to encounter the hanging body of Nicole on my own, and, besides, he was dying with curiosity to find out where I lived and why. I ran up the stairs, knocking everything out of my way.

The flat door was open and the juggler said she wasn't going in. Margo stayed to console her and Anri and I entered, brave and heroic.

Nikipore was standing with headphones on in front of the tape recorder, and since the cable was short and did not allow her to move very far, she was standing on the spot wiggling her bum. I smacked her bottom, and perhaps nobody had ever hit her like that. I probably had such a furious expression on my face that she wasn't even able to remonstrate with me. She explained to me miserably that it wasn't permitted to listen to loud music after eleven o'clock, but she wanted to dance, so she left the door open for them to come in. She had forgotten that there was a lock on the outside entrance. Nicole was very sorry.

The juggler girl had an expression on her face that looked like disappointment. She thought suicide would be really something, but what sort of something, I don't know. She herself was very wealthy. Her grandfather got rich during the Second World War by sending Jews to Switzerland and keeping their wealth for himself. Well, either he sent them, or they went off their own accord, and they might have been lucky and survived, or not. It seems that, in the end, the granddad felt some pangs of conscience and hanged himself in Central Park. After the beloved granddad, her grandmother committed suicide too, not that man's wife but another grandmother. What her problem was I don't know, but after that, it was the turn of the juggler's father, and then her brother. Her mother didn't manage to kill herself—she died from cancer and so was a black spot on the face of the family. The juggler girl was striving to continue the honourable line of her ancestors, but she found it difficult, because she was young, beautiful, rich, and talented. Here were so many things in the way of her ultimate happiness!

When I met her she told me that, although her current

boyfriend seemed to be a nice guy, he wasn't entirely a nice guy. And Ian, well, you haven't seen Ian. She has more than seen him, and even drank beer with this Neanderthal, with his dirty nails and greasy hair. He wiped his nose on his hand and he spoke to her in his horrendous accent about *Madame Bovary*, this Ian with his fourth-class education. Apparently, though, sex with this sub-human creature was amazing. As the juggler was telling us this story, she exposed her breasts, showing scratches all over them. I felt sick.

Now this girl was quietly groaning in the kitchen. Margo was consoling her. Anri was trying to find something to drink in the fridge, but in vain, so he went out to the Turkish shop to get something. Nick was pacing up and down and lamenting, saying that she was useless, ugly, talentless, and a piece of scum. In order to give herself a break, she was saying that, for someone who had been brought up in a family such as hers, she wasn't so bad. It was her rotten, most rotten grandfather who was to blame for everything, this grandfather of hers shouldn't have been buried twice, she said, but never buried at all, just thrown away and left to rot. To hell with his soul—let him die a dog's death.

I, in my stupidity, thought I would neutralize the situation and, totally naively, asked her what she meant by burying her grandfather twice. That was a big mistake. Nikoliko went totally ape-shit, and I'm sure the neighbours would have preferred to hear the music. The juggler's eyes lit up with glee, and that's when I remembered the term, 'necrophilia.'

Her grandfather, apparently a decent Catholic, a doctor, and the hope of the nation, was already married when he fell in love with Nick's grandmother, also a religious and highly virtuous person. The result of this sublime love was Nick's mother, whom I know very well. She's stupid and selfish. The girl was buried deep in the countryside, so as not to sully the doctor's good name, and also for the woman to be safe. The woman was apparently very religious, or else it would have been no problem to get rid of the child. No, not only did she not deprive the child of its life, but she was such an attentive mother that every Christmas and Easter she sent her child presents, such as teddy bears, ribbons, dolls, sweets, in short, everything that a little girl could possibly need. Then her child's father died. I am going to say it again, to hell with his soul. He was buried in the proper way as a good Catholic. They put him in his grave and they threw soil on his coffin. That should have been that; but no, his lover, who was equally religious, bribed a priest and undertaker. The man was dug up, put in the cathedral, and the woman mourned him, and he was buried again. That was that. Now the story's finished.

The put-upon Anri caught the finale of this story, too, as he brought in some beer. My delightful, healthy, tall, one-quarter-Iranian Anri! I thought, to hell with it, I will go out with him tonight, we'll buy tequila and we'll drink so much that belly dancing and the like will be nothing in comparison. Anri has wonderful cats by the way. There was a tomato in the fridge. I felt hungry.

Anri decided to entertain the girls. Bless him, he never left me in the lurch. 'Let's go to the disco,' he suggested. Margo said that it wasn't the time to go to a disco, because they were stressed, and that they needed peace and quiet. The juggler looked at Anri, as if he was a muddy pig who understood nothing. Nikoliko kept saying that she had made my life hell, and that she would never forgive herself, ever! She banged a beer can on the table. Never! Anri got irritated and told Nick in his charming voice to keep her arse still, or he would throw her out. Nick, like an insane person, had an unexpected reaction—she calmed down. By that time, she was already looking at my angel with interest. The sun, my sun, Anri!

While accompanying the girls on their way, Anri told a story about two poor students who fell in love with each other. They got married, they had a baby girl, and there was no limit to their happiness. To mark this happiness the parents sent money to the young couple. They decided to buy a pram for the little girl. They left a baby with the kind old lady next door, and the husband and wife jumped on their motorcycle. They took off, and, at the very first turning, they hit a lorry and were killed. The little orphan girl grew up, became a woman, met Anri, and fell in love with him. Once, after they'd had the most wonderful sex, and at this my angel's eyes gleamed, she became so annoying that her lover threw her out of the window, from the fourth floor. 'You know my house,' he said turning to me.

'And then?' asked the juggler, her voice trembling with excitement, 'Did she die?'

'No, she survived. At the trial she said that she jumped out herself.'

'How much she must have loved you!'

'No, she just knew that I would kill her.'

That night, Nikoliko and I lay together on the sofa. Nick cried all night long, saying that she was not a human being. The girls left. Anri liked my bed very much, he had a good night's sleep there. In the morning he invited Nick to join us for our traditional supper. Nick is not coming but I will go. What else can I do when it gets dark?

IVETA

I found it difficult to memorise the name of this town until it was explained to me that it meant, 'town with a salt lake.' It's a tiny town on the border of two medium-sized developed countries. At one time the town belonged to one of those countries, at another time, to the other. The language of one country was somehow familiar and intelligible to me. I even thought that I could speak it, and as the inhabitants of that country are cultured people, no one ever told me to shut up. Services are conducted in this language in a red brick cathedral with stained glass windows, which, together with the mineral waters, was among the town's notable landmarks. Clearly, the presence of natural mineral water was the reason for two countries to go crazy, otherwise who would be interested in a 'town with a salt lake.'

There's a lake in the centre of the town, where swans and ducks swim, and I would go there after I'd finished my evening meal in the small house where I lived. The house looked like a train and was situated in the park built around the spa for the thermal springs. It was a ghastly place. I used to invite the respectful society of the ducks and swans to share bread baked by Vika-Victoria. I couldn't eat bread myself because I didn't have a single functioning tooth.

Usually my teeth are not in such a bad state. I was undergoing some treatment for an abscess or some hellish thing, and an unnaturally calm dentist ('open wide, close your mouth, rinse and spit') kept filing my teeth for a month. As a result, I could not eat and became skin and bone, and in sheer rage, I shaved my head with a razor. On the one hand, it wasn't too bad. A person in such a state can be forgiven anything, even if she relieved herself in the street, no one would say a word. But it hurt terribly and I was in a state of great irritability with the pain.

As well as the lake and the cathedral, there was a shop in the centre of town, where I had wanted to buy a pair of shoes during the entire time I was there. I can't remember now what kind of shoes they were, or why I went to that shop at all. There was also a cinema. I went once and watched a very silly movie about someone called Emmanuelle, and there was also a café, where holiday-makers fed their children with ice cream. That was it.

The rest of the town consisted of tidy houses, a cemetery full of angels and flowers, a river, a park, another lake, where it was possible to swim, and a forest. Beyond the forest, there was a huge swamp. I was sorry that nobody would ever accompany me there, and I was kind of scared to go to the forest by myself, and anyway, I'm not at all familiar with the swamp. To cut a long story short, that business about the swamp still niggles me, and I bitterly regret that I never visited it. There's no chance of me getting to that town again, and anyway, what's all this about a swamp, as if I have nothing better to think about. On the other hand, it's still a pity, and I wish I'd seen it.

In summer, the forest was an integral part of my cultural life. It was a very beautiful forest, I don't know why I say 'was,' it probably still is, it's just that I have nothing to do with it any more. It was a coniferous forest, with pure air. There were three cycle paths, five, ten, and twenty-five kilometers long. One of the paths went along the river. I saw a rainbow reflected in that river too. Then the rain started, and it poured without ceasing. I got completely wet through. I remember now that, even though it was the middle of summer, I was wearing a sweater that had been singed on a heater. Well, it really was a rotten climate. That rain drove me mad. It had been falling on my head for an hour. I was walking slowly, the bike was useless, as Iveta said, it was 'a piece of shit without brakes.'

So, here we are—Iveta. A heroine. When I arrived in the town with a salt lake, she came to see me the very next day. She, like myself, had prematurely grey hair and was worn out. She wore some kind of idiotic trousers, as narrow as a bit of intestine. Iveta also found it difficult to live in the park with the squirrels and evening walks. In short, we found each other. However, she didn't do everything I did. She hated bicycles as a matter of principle. She didn't go to the bathhouse and she wasn't keen on the lake either. She said it smelled bad. She was right.

But instead of all the above, she discovered the piano con-certs in the park. They were really nice. Wonderful musicians played, old ladies dressed up in their Sunday best and smiled at us, apples fell from the trees. It just so happened that it rained in August, and after that it rained the whole time, constantly. The sun turned bad and mushrooms grew indoors. I forgot about the forest, the concerts and the lake. All that remained was the bath-house, and Iveta.

In fact, Iveta had two children and an extremely pleasant hus-band, but they lived in a different country and they socialised only on the phone. No, they weren't separated and they hadn't fallen out, that's just the way it was, who knows why. 'You know, my poor husband...' That's how she would start telling stories about her family. They were sad stories, nothing bad was hap-pening, but nothing good was happening either. In comparison with her, I was living in a bed of roses. No one's worries made me suffer and nor did my absence break anyone's heart. So, that's how we used to sit during the humid evenings, me and Iveta, the blue-eyed daughter of a Wehrmachtofficer. We ate bananas stolen from Ralphic's kitchen and told stories about this moun-tain and that valley until, in the park built around the spa for the thermal springs, all the leaves fell from the trees, and all the holidaymakers left the town with a salt lake.

Winter came and, accordingly, I went mad. Well, I can only

take so much. Thousands of troubles followed winter. I fell out with the boss. I went to the capital in an angry state and did all kinds of things that were not worth doing. Inevitably, I ended up penniless there, and with the money I'd collected begging outside the Catholic church, I returned home, to Iveta's. For another week, I had the shakes because of some poison I'd taken, and three times a day I crawled through the wet snow to down gallons of mineral water. I couldn't bear this torture for very long. I gave my boss the finger, said goodbye to Iveta and left the town with a salt lake. Probably forever.

I really had forgotten this story, but I somehow heard that Iveta was still alive. She had left her husband and children, this time for ideological reasons, and remarried. My ex gave me this news. He made the effort to call me, and was not too mean to spend money on a phone call. Bless him. I was very happy that he inquired about me. He told me that he married a girlfriend of mine, and asked me if I remembered Iveta. I remembered her, and very well too. Iveta probably remembered too what I had told her about this fine fellow. In the past, I gave her excellent reports of him, but I hope that Iveta refrained from recounting the stories I had told her. She didn't speak to me herself and probably even reprimanded him for phoning me. She was always senselessly jealous, my beautiful friend, Iveta. Just like me.

WITH LOVE TO THE MAN WHOM
I LOVE THE MOST

Remember this from me: nothing good is happening and nothing good will ever happen.
—Lasha B., Tbilisi, 1999

Perhaps your love, as foretold on the cards, is a karmic love.
—Maia K., Berlin,2000

The specific term, 'ex-whore' or 'former whore' is often used to refer to such women. As you like. To some extent, it's true, as it would be foolish to talk about virtue after thirty years. So, the men of my country try to recreate a murky past.

By the time you get to thirty years of age, you can state, without any inhibitions, 'My life is mine to do with as I please.' When you get past thirty, you want to make the most of everything and you are in a position to do so, but the likelihood that someone would really want you, and would be able to tolerate you, is so slight, that it's not worth even thinking about. Don't get uptight, my love, there's no point.

A relationship between a woman of my age and a man resembles bare-knuckle fighting. There are one or two exceptions, such as men who run off to brothels. They are the ones with enough nous not to have anything to do with the likes of me. It's a total waste of time to try to prove that you want nothing from them. What—money, you say? It's more likely that you will have to wine and dine them and send them home in a taxi, so that they get home safely. Anyway, what about a flat? They don't have their own accommodation. It's more likely that there are a hundred people crowded together when his father decides to set off on his final journey from the four-room flat. There's the sister-in-law living on the veranda who has morning sickness, so you'll wet your knickers waiting for her to come out of the toilet. There's his informer of a grandmother, a pseudo-intelligent former Cheka operative, coughing in a corner. His mother, a former provincial turned city-sophisticate, hates you and asks what this woman is doing with her golden boy. My God!

You moody, miserable son of a peasant, who needs you? Both your mother and your retarded older brother, that guy who used to hang around on the street drinking with his mates, probably told you that a woman over thirty is dangerous and she will take advantage of you. Except it's hard to imagine because your brother's vocabulary is too limited for such an exchange. The man in question could easily be either twenty-five or forty-five years old, but that's neither here nor there as he's still a very delicate creature, whereas a woman over thirty is very dangerous, and to boot, there's no question she's an ex-whore who has been around.

Of course, there are some women who aren't dangerous. Girls, for example, who don't fuck. There are girls who will let you fuck them if you beg for a long time and promise to marry them. What kind of girls do you like? Tall, slim, and I don't know what. To come to the point, if the girl is from a good family, you have to marry her, but after that, representatives of the female gender can be divided into three categories: 'wife,' 'female friends,' (those are the ones who, for some reason, you can't fuck, usually because they are ugly) and finally 'good fucks.' The women in this last category can be taken dancing or to Shindisi to eat *khinkali*—Georgian dumplings. The main thing is that you can fulfil your thoroughly hidden sexual fantasies with these women and then boast about it with your neighbourhood mates. And then you have to kiss my mother with that same mouth! Such women usually surface during the summer when the wives are sent off on holidays.

They pop up not far away, in the *dacha* villages, Tskneti, Kojori, Kikete, and Manglisi. All these are wonderful places with fresh air, half an hour's drive to Tbilisi. (I know one very good driver who reached Bagebi in just seven minutes!) Every three days, they have running water and everything. At the weekend, the father of the family will turn up, bringing a watermelon and his mates, he'll drink and will make good use of his modestly suntanned wife. You should be able to see the line of her suntan between her t-shirt and shorts, so you know she isn't the sort of slut to sunbathe naked. He will shag her in as conventional a way as possible so that she won't make any mistake in the future. In order to protect himself from unhealthy, groundless suspicions that his wife might become over-interested in sex, it's a good idea to bring his pal's wife and kids to the same cottage. Your wife considers your mate's wife to be common, but so what? Of course, you wouldn't allow your wife to invite her own girlfriend to the cottage, for example, the ex-whore, the one who shags all over Europe and Asia! You'll visit that one in Tbilisi, on Tuesday or Wednesday, when you feel up to it, and when she refuses to sleep with you, you'll be convinced once more that she really is an ex-whore, who gives blow-jobs, fuck her mother.

But the man I am going to tell you about has yet to lead such an existence. Don't rush, dear! Obviously everything lies ahead, and, for that, we have all the prerequisites in place. You can't find any fault with his looks and masculine attributes, his profession is also respectable and he is bound to make decent money. He only started work a month ago, and he hasn't yet become debased. He'd still kept his humanity, and alcohol and drugs haven't yet drowned his aspirations. He has a brother too, a nice chap, educated, successful, and well-mannered. The brother asks on the phone, with appropriate suspicion, 'Would you like me to pass on a message?' 'No thank you. Do I need any extra problems?' replies the woman.

It is good to be a man, especially when you are so young and you still believe, dear, that everything is okay and will be okay. Well, look, you have barely spoken two words to this woman, you called her by the name of some other woman, and yet she went to bed with you straight away, and she also told you that you were an extraordinary man. It is also true that she did not completely mean what you wanted to hear from her. She blurted out something about it being 'big and warm.'

But you don't know, dear, that that woman spent the previous night in a flooded tent, and apparently it was cold. You, Hercules, you idiot, you don't know how hard it was for her to get warm in the morning, that before you arrived on the scene, she hadn't had an orgasm for the previous one hundred years, and now she is so pleased that she is ready to sing, 'Mommy, mommy' and 'Here's to Victory Day!'

But who will tell you that, sweetheart?

Then, you bump into that woman by accident, well, you wouldn't phone her, would you? Who is she, anyway? To cut a long story short, you meet her and she takes you home, and so, you do the business, then you have a smoke. Of course, you don't take your trousers off, you just pull them down, you are not the one on the receiving end, are you? You do the business, then you have a smoke. You are suspicious of this woman. Why did she stroke your hair? Is she hoping for something? This is dangerous stuff! So you tell her quickly that you are marrying a lassie—what a word!—that you have a lassie, and she is young and beautiful. Why are you unhappy, you are imagining things, you ex-whore. This ex-whore has some audacity, see what she said! 'Fuck off out of here,' she said. 'Don't be so cheeky, know your place, woman.' There's no point swearing at her, she is an ex-whore after all. Therefore, you will give her a couple of punches, you are convinced it isn't the first time, and she will survive it, and of course you will get away with it again and again. You do the business, then you have a smoke. You do the business and then you have a smoke.

Well, that could have gone on indefinitely, but it's summer now, and that ex-whore is hanging around in the street. She makes money by travelling with suspicious-looking men. She doesn't have a husband, so how can she have holidays in Kiketi and have nothing at all? Who knows when she comes and goes, it's too much to expect you to phone her. And in September, a girl will come from Shekvetili, suntanned, with a three-day temporary tattoo and so on. In fact, it's time to get married. You will have a wife and everything.

But when your wife is pregnant for the second time, in order that the first child does not grow up selfish, you will see a light in that woman's window and you will knock casually on her door. By then, she will already be the age of a character from the Bible, and when she finally gives in to you, you will once again be convinced that she is an ex-whore.

A GUARDIAN ANGEL
AND SIMILAR SPIRITUAL BEINGS

I am not really a big fan of that area, but it's nice there in autumn. And that autumn was especially nice. It was warm, we had money. We could afford to sit in the café on the square in the historical center, near the sentry post, drink plenty of beer, and talk a lot. Both the weather and beer were good.

Besides, I wore new shoes. They were a bit tight, but Nico said that they really suited me, and, considering the fact that he rarely said anything kind, I was very pleased. And to match my new shoes, I also bought new stockings, with lace at the top. Nobody could see the lace, but I knew that it was beautiful, and I thought I was beautiful too, and this feeling was marvellous. I showed Nico my stockings and he told me that they were cool. So, from the topic of the above-mentioned stockings we moved on to Marina and then on to angels.

Nico did not mention Marina, but I know who he would buy stockings for. And apart from Marina, seamed stockings wouldn't suit any of his other women. Marina really had amazing legs. As much as she was moody and bad-mannered, you couldn't deny that, at the same time, she was beautiful. At one stage, Nico introduced her to me in the cellar at an exhibition by some conceptual artist—Nico knows a lot of those kinds of people. Before she could open her mouth, I stared at her in amazement and thought, Well done, mate—getting hold of a woman like that.

A Czech guy with a long nose told me about Marina's and Nico's affair. I learned from that Czech that Marina, after living with Nico for several years, met an Italian pizza chef. She left our golden boy, Nico, and she's now hanging around and getting fat somewhere out in the sticks—but the Italian sticks must still be better than her native Barnaul in Siberia. My heart sank, how could anyone upset such a nice guy as Nico?

Anyway, at the end of October, we sat on the square, surrounded by hungry pigeons, me and Nicolosi. I had put my feet up on a stone pedestal, and Nico was telling me what kind of stockings he had brought from Norway to give to a woman. They were black, silk, and had a seam down the back.

'From Norway?'

'Yes. I was there in March. It was cold. I joined the circus.'

Nico is the least athletic person in the world.

'Why are you laughing at me? I made pancakes on a food stall. Why are you grinning? My blinis were delicious!'

'I believe you.'

So, Nico brought the stockings, but the woman told him that she did not love him anymore. Yes, she did not love him anymore and she told him to go away.

'Then what did you do?'

'Then? I left. I went to the station. I sat on the platform and looked at the clock, waiting for the train to arrive. They arrive very punctually here, and I thought, if I jump five minutes before the train arrives, it won't have time to stop.'

'Don't play silly buggers!'

'I swear on my mother's life,' he said.

'You would have died!'

'Don't play silly buggers!' he said then.

'Are you an idiot?'

'Wait, I'll tell you what happened. At that moment a girl came up and asked me for a cigarette.'

'Well, that doesn't happen here.'

'It was extraordinary, and it all started from there. I thought that the next train would come and I told her that I didn't have a cigarette. I suggested smoking something better and she agreed but suggested that this wasn't the place for it so we should go to her house.'

'Was she a nice girl?'

'I don't know, she was just a girl. I got up and followed her. She said she lived nearby.'

'And then what?'

'Hang on. She took me up to the top floor, and I remember clearly that there was a glass ceiling in the bathroom and huge ferns growing in there. In the morning, she rushed up to me, saying, "Come on." It wasn't her house and she was afraid that the owner would turn up. I couldn't wake up and she was pushing and shaking me. "Go," she said, "and I'll follow you down."'

'Some people have a real cheek.'

'Wait, listen. I went down and stood near the doorway. She didn't come. I waited for her but she didn't come. I went up and knocked. Shit, nothing. I went down again. I waited. I waited for the entire day. Then I went to the station.'

'To jump?'

'No, come on, I'd forgotten about that. I was waiting for her.'

'Did she come?'

'No. She disappeared. I walked around the whole house. It had one exit. She had disappeared.'

It got dark, and then it got cold. We emptied our last glasses without enthusiasm. Then, there was a terrible noise of screeching and banging, I don't know what to call it. The pigeons flew up, flapping their wings.

'What's the matter, haven't you heard that noise before? The banks are closing their underground vaults.'

'And why do they make such a noise?'

'Probably deliberately, in order to please the bourgeoisie. That way they know their money is safe. Money and gold teeth belonging to Jews.'

Of course, when we got up, I snagged my stocking.

'Don't worry, I'll buy you a new pair.'

'Oh, thanks, darling,' I answered.

EXPECTING THE BARBARIANS

I'm grateful to my artist friend for 'The Theory of Barbarians.' He was lucky and it became popular in certain circles. According to this theory, people from Tbilisi don't have long left. New people are deliberately destroying their usual habitat, and, alongside this destruction of their houses and their establishment of new values, the notion of the 'urban Tbilisi-ite' is gradually disappearing, in the sense that one or two remaining Mohicans give it.

The first shock Tbilisians received during the Civil War was the arrival of tents. Not the tents themselves, the dirty mattresses, and the smell of borscht, and lavatories from the Painters' House on Rustaveli Avenue, but the strange people who at that time appeared on Rustaveli Avenue. Where they came from, who they were, and what they wanted, God only knows. No one managed to find out, because they disappeared equally unexpectedly. The city breathed a sigh of relief, but unnecessarily, because those people were not dangerous at all—they weren't superior to the Tbilisians in any way, and accordingly they could not defeat them. Their major opponent appeared later, at the time when the Dry Bridge turned into a flea market in the '90s and the Tbilisians were selling their Saxon porcelain and silver sugar bowls.

So, overall, what does it mean to be from Tbilisi? The old Armenian guy, Zhora, for example, was a Tbilisian; he lived in the district of Vera, where his father had a cobblers near the brick factory, on what's now Belinsky Street. He was approximately one and half meters tall, with bent knees, but he had amazingly long fingers, turned yellow from the cheap Astra cigarettes he smoked.

Zhora loved Stalin. If you told him something nice about Stalin he would throw his head back, lift his finger and mutter sweetly,

'Oh, he knew what was what!' He would say that, 'In Stalin's times, things were in their proper place, and a man was like a man, and a woman like a woman, but now, just see what's happening when you go out on the street.' After each phrase, he added, 'And I'm talking to you!'

At one stage, he was an official driver and he chauffeured a government minister. Then he gave up work, and they nagged him at home, 'Come on, do something!' 'I am a hardworking man,' he would say in Russian, 'You give me some work and I'll do the rest.' In recent years, he didn't leave the house, he stood in front of the door, on the doormat, and, like black people who shake their fingers while rapping, he waved his longest index finger: 'In the past, and I am talking to you, when you peeled a cucumber, the smell reached over there.' He pointed far into the distance. 'There was a permit-system back then. Peasants had to have a permit to live in the city,' Zhora would say. Then, he would address an invisible peasant, 'Hey, you, peasant trader, when it is six o'clock, get out of here, you without your permit!' He would wave his hand. 'Hey, man, who would allow a peasant in the town? And don't even mention … that unmentionable!' He would not mention Khrushchev, because he hated him so much. 'And that street sweeper don't even sweep, the town not clean! And I am talking to you!'

Zhora knew that the most dangerous were those he called the half-wits who got rich. There weren't enough beans to feed them. They wiped their bottoms with leaves. They were country bumpkins. If you gave them a five-room flat, they would still build a lavatory under your nose.

'Then, when Zviad, our first president, come along,' Zhora continued, 'and he says, "Armenian, go away!" Where I go? I here nine generations in the town. You think I arrive yesterday? Why you tell me get out? Ask anyone on Elia Street who Zhora is. They all know me. Now all is demonstrations and what not. I don't want to see. Go on, get out from here! Now!'

***

For a while, the Tbilisians referred to the nouveau riche people, the ones so hated by Zhora, as plebs. That's how they defended themselves. But the Tbilisians could find and less to less to argue with them about.

Let's start with the most painful issue for men: Barbarian women are prettier. They exercise, they wear beautiful and expensive clothes, and, in general, they are more attractive than those Tbilisian women hunting for bargains in the hell of second-hand shops, the ones jostling for communal taxis, burdened by cellulite and their useless intellects. It's clear that Barbarian women are not interested in Tbilisian boys who are 'clumsy catfish.' They need healthy males, or, in other words, according to someone's unjustified snobbish remarks, muscular retards. But what use the old native Tbilisians have for minds that aren't retarded isn't clear. If they are so clever, why are they so poor?

The Barbarians' children are getting the best education. Those intelligent moms might look askance at the long legs, tanned from the solarium, of the Barbarians' wives (they grew so long because of the fall-out from Chernobyl), but their children can't compete with the Barbarosovich children. The latter study harder and rarely have runny noses or tonsillitis. They simply thrive better.

The wretched Tbilisian thinks that it is lower class to sit in a smart car; the fact that he doesn't have one is beside the point. He thinks he should live in an old city with peeling walls. But the truth is that, nowadays, he often ends up in the dreary suburbs of Grmagele and Gldani, in a corner flat, on the eighth floor, because at some stage he forgot that he is so incompetent and tried to get rich from the egg trade, but then, so what? But, on the other hand, he has a Balanchivadze grand piano at home, or a Persian rug spread on the floor, the reason being that he was unable to sell them, although he'd never admit it. He is indignant that foolish people are in positions of power in the government, that journalists are illiterate, and that feral dogs are destroyed. He shares his concerns with others similar to himself, accompanied by the Fortuna radio and cheap vodka. The Barbarian doesn't touch cheap vodka, because he looks after himself. He does not smoke those cigarettes that cost only one *lari* either, and in any case, intends to give up smoking.

The Tbilisian likes the past. Not the old Tbilisi, which he never knew, but the time when someone with a master's degree in science could live perfectly well on his salary and take a trip to Moscow three times a month. Moscow and the Soviets are his big love, but he does not speak about it, only occasionally mentioning them in passing. He thinks that if you don't know the Russian language, you are not a human being. In what language would you read the classics?

The Barbarian does not know Russian and does not read classical writers either, nevertheless he is quite happy, at least happier than the Tbilisians. But his children will know Russian, and if they want, they can learn Swahili too. The Barbarian doesn't have a past, so he can focus on the future. Accordingly, he will have a future unlike my beloved men, who still make up the face of this city for the time being, walking around, sad-eyed, carelessly dressed in their once-expensive trousers.

I hope they will be around for another forty years so I won't witness their disappearance.

DOMBROVSKY

There were five of us working there: Anita who was Swedish; Katrin, German; Aksel, Turkish-German; Dombrovsky, Polish; and me, Georgian.

'I'm really Dombrovska, not Dombrovsky, they simply don't understand that a daughter can have a different surname from her father. It makes a big difference to them whether the ending is 'y' or 'a.' They make life easier for themselves by putting this letter 'y' at the end of everyone's names.'

Our boss was called Erik, a German Jew who had been brought up in the States. He was the most crafty and cunning man. He paid well, but he kept us under his thumb. The only one who could deal with him was Dombrovsky, this tiny, skinny girl. She handled him so well that sometimes I even felt sorry for poor Erik.

'At your age, sir, you should be thinking about a retirement home rather than organising a conference.'

Erik was furious, but couldn't say a word. He went mad silently. Then, he stood up and banged the door. Bang! The door of our room. Bang! His office door. I really didn't want to lose my job.

'You can kiss my arse,' muttered Dombrovsky, and buried her head in her computer. 'Don't worry, he'll be back soon, sidling over here. He'll bring coffee too.'

About five minutes later, we heard Mr Erik's voice:

'Hey, you, Georgian, open the door.'

Just as he couldn't handle the 'a' at the end of Dombrovsky, he didn't bother to remember my complicated Georgian name. But he couldn't open the door himself as he had three coffee cups in his hands and the sugar bowl hanging from his little finger. He knew very well that I didn't take sugar, but nevertheless he flirted with and hassled Dombrovsky.

'When it comes to signing a contract,' Dombrovsky instructed me, 'tell him that you are not going to get married. Or you can tell him that you hate men. Don't tell him that you are a lesbian or he'll get confused. Tell him that, throughout your life, your relationships with men never work out, so to cut it short, you are permanently stressed, and that work is the most important thing in your life.'

I didn't understand.

'I didn't understand anything at the beginning either. This is a rotten country. If you get pregnant during the period of your contract, even if you didn't work, he would have to pay your salary. That wouldn't suit him. That's why he'll do his best to find out what you're intending to do. That's why you have to tell him that you hate men.'

Dombrovsky herself had been with the same man for fourteen years and now she was even marrying him.

'He hired me precisely because I have had only one man for the last century and he did not marry me. He's much better looking than me, and he's also German, and a professor. Erik thought that that professor would never marry me. That's why he was relaxed. Do you have such a man? No. So, do what I say.'

I always did what Dombrovsky told me to do and I never regretted it. It was only in regard to food and drink that our tastes diverged. Once I was foolish enough to buy a cake which she'd recommended. I never ate anything worse.

Dombrovsky wore the same pair of jeans continuously for many years. She only took them off on the days when she was meeting her man. On those days she would turn up in a short dress, colourful stockings, and pointy shoes. Once I told her that she looked better in jeans. 'I know,' she said. 'Simply put, he doesn't like jeans, so what can I do? He says I look like Jane Birkin.' Dombrovsky also had thin, crooked legs.

But I liked her in jeans more. When I think of her, I always imagine her sitting on the backless stool with her little bottom, the size of a fist, sticking out. Dombrovsky had very beautiful eyes.

Aksel, the German Turk, was head over heels in love with her. He loved her so much that he was ready to do anything for her. As well as being at work with her all day, he rented a flat with her too. Dombrovsky had two rooms in the right-hand wing, and the left side was Aksel's. Since the time Dombrovsky and Aksel moved in together, Aksel hadn't had a girlfriend. He told me about it himself in the kitchen of that flat.

There were things there belonging to Aksel. A big portrait of Che Guevara hung on the wall and there was a picture painted by Dombrovsky of rather doubtful quality. Aksel boiled spaghetti and opened a bottle of horrible African wine. That's when he told me his story.

'I like blondes. Big women. What can I do about it? I'm Turkish and I like women who are, well, like Pamela Anderson. I never liked women like you and Dombrovsky, skinny as sticks.'

'Thanks, Aksel.'

'Don't be so touchy. You shouldn't get offended. German men will like you, someone like Dombrovsky's professor.'

'Thank you, Aksel.' This time, I meant it whole-heartedly. That professor was a very pleasant man.

'Yes, and you'll like men like him. And Dombrovsky does too. But me, I've been crazy about Dombrovsky for five years, from the day she first came to Erik's. She thought she looked great when she wore these jeans and a white shirt. She wore a silk shirt, can you imagine?'

I got rather worried. I sometimes wore a silk shirt too. I wondered what was wrong with a silk shirt.

'When you wear a silk shirt, and it's also white, you shouldn't wear a red bra underneath. Especially when you don't have any breasts. Remember that from me.'

Ouch. He treated us like scum.

Dombrovsky was less interested in such things. She was mainly interested in money. She had a portrait of Coco Chanel in her room. It was a cool photo. Dombrovsky considered Coco Chanel the coolest woman in the world.

'Coco said that it wasn't money that excited her, but the freedom she bought with that money. That's so cool, isn't it?'

Dombrovsky was born in Socialist Poland, in a village called Mikołajki. In comparison to her background, it was as if I came from Miami Beach. Her father bred rabbits. Back then, Dombrovsky only knew one language, Polish, and even that, she told me, she knew badly, because she did not read books or watch TV. Only one woman in that village had a television, and she and her mother had fallen out. When Dombrovsky graduated from school, members of the Dombrovsky family got together and had a meeting. After the meeting, her father called and spoke to her. Dombrovsky told this story in an engaging manner.

Her father said to her, 'Pani Dombrovska, we've decided that you have to go.' The Dombrovskys pooled their money and sent the best representative of their family to Germany to study.

Even the most desperate Georgian immigrants don't settle in the town where Dombrovsky ended up. If I translate Dombrovsky's description of the town word for word, it would be 'the arsehole of the world.' There, Dombrovsky looked after one daft child and studied German. Then she moved to a slightly bigger town and entered the Arts College. She wasn't very good at painting, but she was even more hopeless at anything else. She used to say that she had two left hands. It was there she met her professor.

'I know why this prick of a professor went mad,' Aksel told me, 'because, in this rotten country, no one ever had a chance to have a virgin. That slime ball has been torturing that poor girl and stripping her of her soul for ten years.'

Dombrovsky did not seem to be stripped of her soul. While Aksel and I were drinking African wine, she went to the dress-maker's to try on her wedding dress.

'Yes, now he is marrying her. Because he's got old and he wouldn't be able to find somebody like Dombrovsky in Canada, the prick.'

The day before the wedding, apparently there was some kind of traditional gathering. Poor Aksel found himself adopting the status of a family friend, and, together with the professor, ended up at a stag night. Dombrovsky came round to my place by bicycle and we women went out together. Naturally, on the way, her wheel got stuck in the tram tracks, and both Dombrovsky and her bicycle fell on me. 'Poor you.' Dombrovsky was worried. 'Poor old you.' At the same time, she was brushing the dirt off her jeans and mine. She was always doing some kind of damage to me like that. She poured coffee all over me, and twice I was in a car accident because of her. When she helped to decorate my flat, she splashed me. Thank God it was the traditional Soviet flour and water glue, so I was spared having to shave my head.

That night our girl got pissed. She stood on the table singing, 'Poland will never die!' and she was swearing that when she married him, then she will cheat on him at last.

On her wedding day, Dombrovsky looked very beautiful, more beautiful than anyone else. They had the wedding on an island in the lake. Aksel had to stay until the morning because there was no ferry, so the bride booked a room for him in a small hotel. Mr Erik stayed too, he drank Russian vodka and lamented the loss of his employee. When Dombrovsky threw her bouquet of flowers, I caught it. I can overpower German women at least.

The professor's mother wore a pink, transparent dress and her red bra was visible. I caught Aksel's eye. 'Why are you looking at me? Can't you see what big breasts she has?' Poor Aksel.

Polish people turned up at the wedding, too. The only Dombrovsky who knew German, called for attention and raised a glass:

'Pani Dombrovska,' he began, 'now you are going to a faraway country. When you arrive there, they will certainly ask you where you came from. If you tell them what your homeland is called, they may not understand. That's why you must tell them, "I am from the country where children are not forbidden to make a noise in the afternoon, and dogs are not forbidden to bark at night, and I am from the country where old people in the backyard tell their children about their love affairs." You tell them that! "I am from the country where storks greet spring by tapping their beaks, and in winter, the moon illuminates the road for travellers." And then everybody will understand that you were born in Mikołajki.'

Many years have passed since then. I miss Pani Dombrovska a lot.

WHICH MADATOV?

A very clever man, Mr Borislavsky, a Ukrainian who had been living in Georgia for fifteen years, diagnosed the inhabitants of Tbilisi as people with an 'unrestrained tendency towards myth creation.' He said Georgians had a very interesting attitude towards time. I don't mean habitually being late and such like. For example, I was once told a story about a church in Svaneti which Zakaria-the-Long-Armed asked the monk, Teophane, to build. The story-teller's grandfather, who is around sixty years old, also took part in the construction of the church. The architect was Momi Chegiani, a participant of the nineteenth-century rebellion in the village of Khalde, and as for the monk, Teophane, his descendants have his photograph in their homes, but that's not important. What are one, two, three or four centuries in comparison with eternity?

I should tell you that such things don't only happen in the highlands of Svaneti. Today, even in our era of egg-headed computer specialists and the nuclear bomb, they tell remarkable stories in Tbilisi too. One such story concerns the Madatov house.

Anyone who has ever walked through the old district of Sololaki will know this house. It is the one with a tower.

It is a very beautiful house. In my childhood I was convinced that it was the biggest house in the world. It has huge rooms and in every room there are fireplaces up to the ceiling. These fireplaces are different in each room and profusely decorated. The whole universe is depicted on them, including men, women, various kinds of vases, and flowers. The house has fabulous balconies, the residents grow roses there, you can sit there in an armchair surrounded by roses and gaze and gaze at the rocks of the Botanical

Gardens. No, I'm lying, you can't anymore. Now, they are building some tall buildings and the view is spoiled.

However, the gardens remain as they always were. Whoever designed the house was an expert at his job. Apparently, there were pools in the gardens before. Now, of course, they've gone, but, nevertheless, the area is still very beautiful. The entrance hall has paintings and one glass wall. Now the paintings are in a bad state and the glass wall no longer lets the light in, but when you are a small girl and your father takes you to the cinema to see *Angelique Marquise des Anges* you immediately imagine the epoch of princesses. You walk down the wide marble staircase rustling your silk dress. And from the entrance hall, you descend the stairs, which are also decorated, to the garden, and reach the trellis work and look over to Chonkadze Street, where a prince mounted on his white horse is surely waiting for you.

The story of the address of this house has always been lost in the mists of time. It is number 4, Chonkadze Street, and also number 10, Gergeti Street. This is the least of its problems. In fact, on the contrary, it's fun when one house has two addresses. It got somewhat difficult, though, when there was a conversation about the builder and the owner of the house.

Sololaki people are unanimous in one thing. The house with the tower is certainly the Madatov House. And they tell incredible stories about it.

The Georgian Encyclopaedia doesn't mention Madatov. It only refers to Madatov's Island. Apparently, General V. Madatov bought an island in the nineteenth century, and that's why it was called M.I. (that is to say, Madatov's Island). That's all.

I decided, even with my limited wits, that I knew something. This V. Madatov's first name was Valerian, but he was also known as Rustam. He was the son of Gregory Madatov, who was a Lieutenant General and a hero of the war of 1812. He originated from Karabakh. I read that he was born in 1872 and was orphaned at a young age. His Uncle Jemshid, the Governor of Karabakh, took him to St Petersburg when he was aged fifteen.

The Armenian, Prince Valerian Madatov, got on well with the Russian officers. He fought courageously and received the third and fourth Orders of the Cross of St George and two gold swords for bravery. The first was awarded for his part in the war with the Turks, and the second, for the war with the French. His contemporaries described him as an 'unbelievably fearless General' but Denis Davidov, the Russian soldier-poet of the Napoleonic wars, insinuates that he wasn't a prince at all, that he had his mother's surname, and, at one stage, he was accused of being homosexual, but this had no impact on his courageousness. Besides, he was married to the beautiful daughter of General Sablukov, and it's not possible a woman like her would have married a useless man.

Let's continue. From 1816, under the auspices of General Yermolov, Prince Madatov was working for the public good in the Caucusus. He fought and worked to maintain peace for the mountain people. When the Russian-Iranian war began, Madatov was summoned to Tbilisi. That was during the period 1826-1828. Pay attention, those dates are important!

I won't bore you with the last stretch of General Lieutenant Valerian, son of Gregory, Madatov's life. I'll spare you accounts of why Count Paskevich sent him to the home front, or why Madatov went to St Petersburg, and where else he fought, and so on. It's not my intention to tell these stories. The main thing is, that in 1829 he died from consumption, and is now buried in the Alexander Pechersk Lavra in St Petersburg, and his portrait hangs in the Military Gallery of the Winter Palace.

Clearly, I concluded that the house must have belonged to this particular Madatov, if it was any Madatov's, when suddenly, out of the blue, another Madatov turned up. He also had the initial V. and was born in the nineteenth century. He was not a general but he was an industrialist. He lived towards the end of the nineteenth century, by which time the other brave general had been long dead. Apparently, the house must have been built by the industrialist because the general had no need of such a big house when Sololaki belonged to him, so they told me. They also told me that the Sololaki district belonged to Armenians, and what else could I imagine?

I would like to tell you that I haven't come to any conclusions at all, because a third Madatov turned up as well. He was called Rostom, which means his initial is R. and not V., and just when I thought I finally knew who the true builder of the house was, I was reminded by someone that Valerian was also known as Rustam. So what's the difference between Rostom and Rustam? They diligently took me to the Public Library, and there I read that Rostom Madatov, Mirzajana, was of course Armenian by origin but he was born in Azerbaijan (and even today I couldn't tell whether Karabakh is Armenian or Azeri). It goes without saying that he lived in Georgia, and he even wrote poems. His friends in Georgia included many poets and public figures, such as Grigol and Alexander Orbeliani, Giorgi Eristavi and David Korganashvili. If he was friendly with such highly esteemed people—to employ Tbilisi-style logic—why would anyone give Madatov an island? And that poor chap was a military person as well, not quite a General, but a Colonel, and then what? If one hundred years means nothing for us, some kind of meaningless rank isn't worth talking about! All this was happening in the nineteenth century to Rostom or Rustam, but the fact is Madatov died in 1837. In short, I got tied up in a great muddle, but never mind, no big deal!

V. Madatov had a daughter, who died very young from consumption. Her grief-stricken father buried her in the cemetery above that house. Nobody remembers there being a cemetery there, but that doesn't necessarily mean anything. In order to be able to see his daughter's tomb, he commissioned an Italian architect to construct a tower on the house. Look, the department store on

Plekhanov Street has a similar dome, and what do you think, who built that? As for consumption, it appears to be a genetically transmitted disease, and so we can assume that the woman must have been the daughter of Madatov, because the General died from consumption too.

Here's Version Number Two: V. Madatov had a daughter who had consumption. We already know that. But according to this version, that Madatov was not General Madatov; rather he was married to a General's daughter and he wouldn't permit his daughter to marry some wealthy market-trader (that was the word the boys hanging around in the street used, much to my surprise) like Khenuntsi, would he? Okay. When all's said and done, Khenuntsi loved his wife very much and after the wedding he took her to Switzerland for treatment. Then he got caught up in the 1917 Revolution, and that's why they didn't return. They stayed in Switzerland and died there. The house was left without an owner and that's why, ultimately, thirteen families moved in. Lieutenant-General Madatov (the one who died in 1829) was not the kind of man to have let anyone into his house. They didn't call him 'Bloody Madatov' for nothing!

So here's the conclusion: Madatov's daughter would have been born in 1830 at the latest, which that means that in 1917, Khenuntsi was in love with an eighty-seven-year-old woman. He took this old woman for treatment, not to some miserable spa in Georgia, like Abastumani, but directly to Switzerland.

And then, like the Madatovs, the Khenuntsis multiplied too. Although Khenuntsi appeared to remain in Switzerland, he also kept pigeons in the tower of the Madatov house after the time when the house was converted into communal apartments. Yes, he lived in Switzerland but at the same time he lived in the tower together with his pigeons and turtle doves.

***

I have personally stopped poking my nose into the history of the Madatovs. I'm afraid that I may too start multiplying, double or triple myself, and end up following in the footsteps of some Sololaki people, by announcing that, although Madatov was childless, he was still my grandfather. What happened in reality they can find out more easily without me, if they still are able to ferret around in the archives with three Madatovs and two Khenuntsis, and if they don't bore everyone to death with foolish questions, such as, 'Who was that?' and 'What was he doing there?' But what does it matter which Madatov built this little palace? The main thing is that he built it very well and it is enough for me that, with the help of God, I can visit one of the most beautiful houses in Tbilisi.

THE PARADISE OF THE COMMUNAL FLAT

I, too, grew up in a *communalka*, a communal apartment on Vo-
rontsov Street, around an Italian-style courtyard, on the second
floor. Several of us families shared a kitchen and a toilet, there
was no such thing as a bathroom. We used the kitchen for bath-
ing and would close the door, knowing it would be exactly at that
moment someone would want to make tea or wring out their
washing.

Of course, communal flats existed outside Tbilisi, but the
Tbilisi *communalka* had a special charisma, at least because of its
multi-cultural (and not internationalist) character. There's nothing under the sun that you won't see here. Why do we need glo-
balisation, my dear friends, when Tbilisi *communalka* still exist?

While I lived there, I spoke excellent Kurdish, and I could
make out quite a bit of Armenian. An Armenian guy, Gurgen
Petrovichi, used to take me into his room, which was always dark
for some reason, and was free of the usual noise of a mixture of
music for belly-dancing or for Kurdish weddings. Everything he
had, from the chandelier to the teaspoon, was exquisitely beautiful and, as I now realise, very expensive. Before the revolution, the
old man had been a very high up member of a merchants' guild
and the owner of a hotel. He would take me into his strange
room, pour me a cup of strong and frothy tea. He would say that
only plebs drank sweet, weak tea, and he used to explain to me:
'hats' means 'bread,' 'jur,' 'water.' When I attempted to say something in my pitiful Armenian, he interrupted me immediately.
Apparently only very low-class people spoke Armenian so poorly,
and that kind of language had the smell of the street. And so that
he would not think that I was plebeian, I slurped the black tea

in a panic and listened to him in silence when he talked about which kind of diamonds were good and which were not so good. But, as a result, and I'm even now quoting that old gentleman, Gurgen, word for word, perhaps people can be fooled and think that I really do deal with diamonds all the time.

As well as Gurgen Patrovichi, we had a lot of other interesting neighbours. I have especially fond memories of one of them, the fattest and most bad-tempered of all, who used to destroy swallows' nests with a broom, but in vain—they kept coming. 'They flap around and produce droppings,' he used to say. He himself happily washed his yellow chamber pot at the only tap, and there was an incredible lamenting and cursing in the kitchen, in Georgian, Armenian, Russian, and occasionally in German too, when the poor German, who lived on the floor below, decided to drink tea and speak about bringing up problems with the neighbours.

This sink had one extraordinary feature, there was always something blocking it, sometimes cherry stones, sometimes tea and the water kept leaking. The downstairs neighbour, a man who wore a stocking on his head, would rush upstairs to kill someone on our floor, he was so angry. Anyway, that guy was always angry. He was forever yelling at his grandchild in a terrible voice. 'Come here and I will kill you with a beating,' he would shout. Once, at night, when everyone had gone to sleep, one of the neighbours decided to develop and print some photographs. One photo fell into the above-mentioned sink, and of course it got wet and got stuck to the plug hole. The tap continued to drip in the silence of the night, and the man continued his business happily by the red light, until he found that everything had gone totally wrong. There was a puddle in the kitchen and then the neighbour arrived! But living in a *communalka* is a great education. The man walked in wet shoes along the corridor up to his door, and after that he took his shoes off, and, in his stocking feet, disappeared into his room. The neighbour who rushed from the floor below followed the wet foot prints and found him there. Even I remember the horrible scandal that you would only wish on your worst enemy.

On the whole if you ignore the continuous arguments, where if you participate less you get even more furious—which is why it's always better to express yourself—and if you can ignore the disapproving glances and loud whispers about morals in relation to 'some people,' then living in the *communalka* can be priceless.

The house I am telling you about now is a wonderful house. Today, it is in the center of the town, but, probably at some stage, it was in some wretched area. I personally would never be happy to live near a cemetery. Now that cemetery no longer exists. If it ever existed, we knew nothing about it. It was the neighbour next-door who told us about it, and who had lived in this house at that time. She seemed to be the age of Methuselah. She couldn't read or write, apart from her signature, and she knew the Lord's Prayer in Latin, only she did not remember that she knew it in Latin. To cut things short, it was all very confusing. This good woman had been in prison at some stage. She herself claimed that she was sent to prison because she was a supporter of Trotsky, but wagging tongues, in other words the neighbours, argued that she was in prison because she had murdered her second husband. That poor man got drunk and stood in the window, the one from which she now throws gnarled bones to the cats. She grabbed his legs and threw him out. Before that she had killed the first husband by smothering him with a pillow, and now her sins had caught up with her.

These last words, about sins, were worth thinking about, because at nights this virtuous old lady, once a month at least, beat herself against the walls of her twelve-meter-square room. Incomprehensibly to me, but comprehensibly to her other neighbours, she shouted in some kind of Jewish language, 'Let me go, let me go!' Her cries were echoed by the howling of the spaniel, which was stupefied by tranquilizers given to him to subdue his mating urges, and by my friend's shouting, 'Ouch, help me, I'm going mad!' But, on the other hand, after such a night everyone found it difficult to get up, and in the morning, the usual shouts of 'Hey, your tea is getting cold,' and the shuffling sound of the sleepers didn't wake us up, and we'd sleep soundly.

Then the old lady died, and after some shifting to and fro, a lady called Sima added the old lady's room to her own. It seemed she was too lazy to cook in the communal kitchen, that's why, on the days when her son and daughter-in-law came to visit her, and she lit up her kerosene stove in the room, there was a horrendous smell in the entrance. At first we thought she was boiling a cat, but apparently not; she was preparing *dolma*, stuffed cabbage leaves. The smell of kerosene and pickled cabbage in the barrel in the corridor did not go well together. At such times we usually burnt a newspaper in the room and everything was fine again.

That burning of a newspaper led to a disaster for my friend. Besides, she was blonde, with some Russian parentage, she had blue eyes, and also she was afraid of fights, and that's why she usually quietly slipped away. Besides, she smoked. Once God got angry with her and she rushed to the toilet in her underwear. Everything was over and it was decided that she was practicing black magic and worse, and of course she was immoral. But in reality, all she did was secretly steal cutlets from a neighbour's frying pan, and also she helped herself to half of Babkena's barrel of pickles, but nobody noticed. People are daft. Certainly they did not speak to this wretched woman until one winter, when water, gas and light went off simultaneously, and this poor girl instructed them that, on the other side of the street, near the small garden, that there was an excellent public toilet and that she would boil water to make tea for them, and that she had a cast-iron pan and a decorated teapot.

In those days I understood for the first time what community meant, what love is, how to live as one and how nice it is when there's no distinction between rich and poor. Well, I wish only wealthy people existed. That weak, sweet tea was disgusting, plebeian, in fact.

GEORGIAN LITERATURE SERIES

The Georgian Literature Series aims to bring to an English-speaking audience the best of contemporary Georgian fiction. Made possible thanks to the financial support of the Georgian National Book Centre and the Ministry of Culture and Monument Protection of Georgia, the Series began with four titles, officially published in January 2014. Available in January 2015 are four new titles, offering readers a choice of Georgian literary works.

www.dalkeyarchive.com

GEORGIAN LITERATURE SERIES

Erlom Akhvlediani
Vano and Niko & other stories / Translated by Mikheil Kakabadze
Akhvlediani's minimalist prose pieces are Kafkaesque parables presenting individual
experience as a quest for the other. ISBN 978-1-62897-106-4 / $15.95 US

Lasha Bugadze
The Literature Express / Translated by Maya Kiasashvili
The Literature Express is a riotous parable about the state of literary culture, the
European Union, and our own petty ambitions—be they professional or amorous.
ISBN 978-1-56478-726-2 / $16.00 US

Zaza Burchuladze
adibas / Translated by Guram Sanikidze
A "war novel" without a single battle scene, Zaza Burchuladze's English-language
debut anatomizes the Western world's ongoing "feast in the time of plague."
ISBN 978-1-56478-925-9 / $15.50 US

Tamaz Chiladze
The Brueghel Moon / Translated by Maya Kiasashvili
The novel of the famous Georgian writer, poet and playwright Tamaz Chiladze
focuses on moral problems / issues, arisen as a result of the too great self-assuredness
of psychologists. ISBN 978-1-62897-093-7 / $14.95 US

Mikheil Javakhishvili
Kvachi / Translated by Donald Rayfield
This is, in brief, the story of a swindler, a Georgian Felix Krull, or perhaps a cynical
Don Quixote, named Kvachi Kvachantiradze: womanizer, cheat, perpetrator of
insurance fraud, bank-robber, associate of Rasputin, filmmaker, revolutionary, and
pimp. ISBN 978-1-56478-879-5 / $17.95 US

Zurab Karumidze
Dagny
Fact and fantasy collide in this visionary, literary "feast" starring historical
Norwegian poet and dramatist Dagny Juel (1867-1901), a beautiful woman whose
life found her falling victim to one deranged male fantasy after another.
ISBN 978-1-56478-928-0 / $15.00 US

Anna Kordzaia-Samadashvili
Me, Margarita / Translated by Victoria Field & Natalia Bukia-Peters
Short stories about men and women, love and hate, sex and disappointment, cynicism
and hope—perhaps unique in that none of the stories reveal the time or place in they
occur: the world is too small now for it to matter. ISBN 978-1-56478-875-7 / $15.95 US

Aka Morchiladze
Journey to Karabakh / Translated by Elizabeth Heighway
One of the best-selling novels ever released in Georgia, and the basis for two feature
films, this is a book about the tricky business of finding—and defining—liberty.
ISBN 978-1-56478-928-0 / $15.00 US

www.dalkeyarchive.com